ALL THE
OLD BARGAINS

Leo Haggerty Novels by Benjamin M. Schutz

EMBRACE THE WOLF
ALL THE OLD BARGAINS
A TAX IN BLOOD (Fall 1986)

Published by Bluejay Books

ALL THE
OLD BARGAINS

Benjamin M. Schutz

BLUEJAY BOOKS INC.

A Bluejay Book, published by arrangement with the Author.

Copyright © 1985 by Benjamin M. Schutz

Jacket art by Jill Bauman

Book design by James Frenkel

Manufactured in the United States of America

First Bluejay printing: September 1985

Library of Congress Cataloging in Publication Data

For my sons,
Jakob and Jesse,
who give me so much more
than I ever bargained for

Acknowledgments

The author would like to thank the following people for the gracious donation of their expertise: Officer Adam Schutz, MPDC; Mark Schutz, M.D.; Neil Ruther, attorney-at-law; Sharon Fitch, ACSW, Supervisor, Fairfax County Child Protection Service Treatment Team; Jim Holliday, Steven Spruill and Steve Thomas, friends and fellow writers; Betty Paul; Marsha Barton-Hyde.

"Realized he had made all the old bargains human life is based on: To give the cool or angry young a father, the target that won't shoot back. To stand by a friend in trouble, even when the friendship ended, because [that's] what being friends implied . . . To carry the woman, if she failed, because she'd carry you if she could. Not to take advantage of a child's love."

VANCE BOURJAILY
Brill Among the Ruins

ALL THE
OLD BARGAINS

Chapter 1

I ENJOY THE DRIVE DOWN THE PARKWAY, THE CUPOLA OF TREES overhead, the river running alongside, the crisp sails of the boats in the marina. I turned into Belle Haven and began to wind up the hill. The large houses were set back from the street and each other. I found the Bensons' and turned into the driveway. It was a large square colonial, white, two stories. The pillared front porch was edged by the pink splash of flowers. Sometimes I think it's against the law to build anything but a colonial in Virginia. But then again that was Virginia's golden age.

I got out of my car, glanced around the side of the house and then down the street. I went up the steps and rang the door bell. There was, thank god, no black jockey by the door. The door was opened by a woman who seemed roughly my age. Her close-cropped hair, unmade face and simple black dress impressed me as self-denial, not stylish restraint. She looked at me through out-of-focus vacant eyes as if she had been withdrawn deep in thought and the door bell had just recalled her to the surface world. "Yes?" She winced and her eyes blinked rapidly as if she expected me to hit her.

"I'm Leo Haggerty. Are you Mrs. Benson?"

"Yes. Please come in." She quickly stepped back to let me pass. Her eyes darted up and down the block to check if anyone else had seen me arrive. I thought about telling her I'd had all my shots, but a moment of maturity prevailed.

I followed her through a dark corridor into the living room. The back wall was glass, overlooking a pool. To the left was an ample wet bar. We sat on the sofa around a Noguchi coffee table. I looked over to her for a moment to see if she could start to tell

1

me what the problem was but she looked at me dumbly. Her mind seemed frozen by confusion and embarrassment. I always bring out the best in people.

"Mrs. Benson, what can I do for you?"

Mrs. Benson looked everywhere but at me. The answer was not on the ceiling. It was not out in the pool. With a forlorn sigh she found it in her lap.

"It's my daughter Miranda. She's run away. I want you to bring her back."

"What makes you think she's run away?"

Finally she looked at me. "Don't they all these days? She thinks she's all grown-up, let me tell you. She's doing badly at school, doesn't mind her father or me, comes in when she wants to, does what she wants to. Quite a mouth on her too. The things that come out of it. Her contempt for everything we've done and tried to give her."

"How long has this been going on?"

"Since she entered junior high school. Before then she was an angel, daddy's little girl and all that. It's like she changed when she went there, like something poisoned her."

"How long has she been gone?"

"Since yesterday. She didn't come home from school. She didn't call."

"Have you called the police?"

"Called the police! I'm taking a chance talking to you."

"How so?'

"My husband. He's out looking for Miranda now. He was out last night and earlier this morning too. He'd have a stroke if he knew I told anyone about this."

"Then why have you?"

"To find my daughter. He won't."

She seemed to have struck a balance between fear of her husband's rage and contempt for him. So she'd hire me but behind his back. How big a part of the decision was concern for her daughter I couldn't tell.

"Going back to her running away, why do you think she would do that?"

"Who knows. She doesn't tell me anything. We're the enemy. How we got that way I don't know."

"Do you have a picture of her? I'm going to need a current one, a list of her friends, and a letter from you authorizing me as your agent."

"We don't have a recent picture of her. She refused to have it taken at school, and who her friends are these days I don't know."

"Did she say why she didn't want her picture taken?"

"Yes. It was something cute and witty and so grown-up, like 'evil is in the eye of the beholder.'"

A dark stream ran between mother and daughter. It was brackish with resentments that were too old or too deep to clean.

"Let me have the latest photo of her and a list of her old friends."

She got up from the sofa and went down the hall. I watched her leave the room, moving in mechanical precision, as if she were trying to walk without moving anything except her legs. She stole a glance at me over her shoulder as she passed the mirror.

I was lost in my thoughts, following her down the dim corridor, when the front door slammed and jerked my head around. He steamed into the living room, head lowered like a rhinoceros. When he came to a halt he picked his head up and blinked, as if he only knew I was there by smell.

He squared up to me. "Who are you?" I got up from the sofa. He was a meaty man but running to fat. On his face was one of those waxed handlebar mustaches that look like a bat is sleeping under your nose.

"My name is Leo Haggerty. I'm a private detective."

"She hired you, huh? Well, I fired you. Get out. I can take care of things around here. I don't need your help. Beat it." He gave me the heave-ho with his thumb as if I were attached to it by a line. Mrs. Benson's fear seemed to be getting the best of her. She could not have missed her husband's return. She'd left me here to fend for myself.

I looked down the hall, waiting for her to return. After all, she was my client. I was here at her request. When I'd given her a decent interval to appear and she didn't, I decided to leave. She'd have to do better than this if I was going to put myself out for her.

"If you and your wife get your signals straightened out and want my services, I'm in the phone book." I went past him. He was the picture of suburban success. There was some little animal insignia on everything he wore. I wondered if it was a rhinoceros. I hoped so. I let myself out.

I decided that the view down the hill from here was quite nice: the rolling lawns, old shade trees, the road winding down to the country club in the distance. The view behind the double doors was grim. I wondered if the kid had a good reason to be lost. I doubted I'd ever find out. Things were quiet in the house—no screams, no tinkling crashes, no whip-cracking slaps. I went down to my car.

Backing out of the driveway I found myself without a client and indifferent to that. The publicity generated by the Saunders case had provided me with a steady stream of clients. For the first time I could afford to turn down work. As the sole proprietor of a lovely afternoon, I decided to go to the racquet club, work up a sweat, have dinner out and maybe end up with a good book.

Chapter 2

THE WEIGHT ROOM WAS BEING USED FOR A FASHION SPREAD IN a local magazine. I went back to the front desk to see if any racquetball courts were available. One was, so I took it and headed for the locker room. I no longer play the game seriously or often. Chronic knee and ankle injuries have seen to that. My orthopedist says I will make him a rich man yet.

I changed into my gear and thought about something to work on; judgment, that was what I lacked. I was always trying to do too much with my forehand, always attacking. Like the poster says: Patience my ass, I'm gonna kill something. I made my way up to the courts. They were all lit. I stood in the lounge for a second, watching a pair of older guys move the ball around with finesse and control. I could probably learn more by watching them than by playing myself, but I needed to work out. The morning with the Bensons had left me tense. I wanted to burn that tension out of my system. On another court a husband and wife were playing pitty-pat. The third was empty.

I ducked into the court, dropped the ball and hit a ceiling ball to the front wall. I waited for it to bounce, rise, drop and then let it rip off the front wall to my backhand. I moved over early and set up, turning my shoulders, cocking the wrist, watching the ball, timing the explosion. I moved into the ball, hips sliding, shoulders turning and snapped my wrist, hitting a rocket along the wall; not quite a rollout but better than I had been hitting. I picked up the ball and chanted my mantra: set up early, swing through, snap the wrist. I hoped my motor pathways were listening, letting the soothing sound seep into them, forever changing their structure. I hit a forehand off the front wall

5

toward the side wall. Moving crosscourt I was trying to read whether to pick it off in the air or to let it hit the third wall and try to kill it. I waited, coiling. It hit the back wall and fell toward the floor. I waited and then released. It was maybe two inches off the floor all the way to the wall and intimate with it all the way back. I stooped over to pick up the ball when I heard a tapping on the glass back wall. A woman was pointing toward the door to the court. I nodded and waved her in. She opened the door to the court, ducked and entered.

"Listen, my partner is going to be late, and I saw you were alone. Would you be interested in playing a game?" She cocked her head like a question mark.

She was of average height, and lots of that was leg. Everywhere she was firm and rounded. I thought of Roethke's line: "She had more sides than a seal." Her chestnut hair was in a braided pony tail. But it was her face that transfixed me. The big dark eyes and wide mouth contrasted with the sculpted hollows and planes of her cheeks. It was a face of excess and denial, a face that promised all things.

She cocked her head again. "Well?"

"Uh, oh sure." I felt sixteen again. With women I think I always will. They're still a mystery to me. Maybe I've just been a poor student.

"Let's play here. We'll lob for serve," she said.

"No, you take it." I saw her mouth harden as if I'd insulted her. It was probably foolish of me to play with her. I just needed to work up a sweat, nothing more. I'd take it easy. I set up behind her. She looked back at me to check if I was ready. I nodded. She served a lob into the corner that rattled off the walls like a quarter in a deep pocket. I flicked a backhand toward the ceiling but it was not deep enough. She set, coiled to swing. I moved back to center court next to her, waiting for her to decide where to put it. She chose a kill to my backhand. I dug hard for it but barely got my racket on it. Her point. She was good. Too good for me to beat at less than full speed, if then.

"One serving zero," she said and eyed me for the okay to

serve. I nodded. She went back to the backhand lob. I guessed she would and was early, chanting *set up, set up*. I picked it off the side wall and hit a deep ceiling ball. She retreated, and I entered center court, crouching like a giant toad waiting to gobble the ball as if it were a rubber fly. Her return was short to my forehand side. I sized her up, coming back from the far left corner and waited for the ball to drop, getting ever fatter. I then drilled it into the right corner. Rollout. My serve.

I went to the service court, "zero serving one," and awaited her signal. I hit a drive serve low and to her backhand. She got to it and hit a weak lob to the front court. I waited for the kill and hit a pinch shot off the far wall. My point.

"One serving one." We began again. I hit another drive serve to her backhand. She hit a passing shot down the line. I hit a crosscourt pass. She was there, but she lifted her return. Dinnertime for froggy! She came back to center court. I hit my pass behind her.

"Damn," she said and grimaced. "Nice shot."

We set up again, but as I looked back, I saw another woman knocking on the glass back wall.

"Is that your partner?" She looked up and nodded.

"Well, I enjoyed it. Uh, by the way, I'm Leo Haggerty, and you're—?"

"Samantha Clayton, and I enjoyed it too."

She turned and walked off the court. I watched her volleying hips as she left. I finished my workout and left the court. I showered and shaved and headed out to the lobby, wondering where to eat. As I walked across the lobby I saw her fishing in her purse for phone money. I crossed to her. I thought about my father's putting motto: never up, never in. It always worked better with golf.

"Uh, excuse me. Would you care to have dinner with me?"

She looked at me with those big eyes and cocked her head to one side. A characteristic motion. I hoped she graded on a curve. She nodded and said okay.

7

I asked her if she liked seafood and she said yes. I asked her if she'd ever eaten at Crisfield's. She said no.

Since a friend had dropped her at the club we got into my car and headed toward the beltway. She was watching me as I drove.

"Do you play often?" she asked.

"No. I usually lift weights here, but today the weight room was occupied."

"Oh, I work out here too. Usually in the afternoon. I've never seen you here."

"When I come it's usually first thing in the morning. But it's erratic; my hours aren't real regular."

"What do you do in those irregular hours?"

"I'm a private investigator. And you?" We were volleying, hitting ceiling balls. Keep it high. Wait for the other person to commit.

"I'm a writer."

"Oh, what kind of stuff?"

"You name it. Magazine pieces, interviews, literary journal essays, short stories. My first novel will be out soon."

"What is it called?"

"No Snake in the Garden."

"When is it due out?"

"A month or two."

"I'll look for it."

She turned partway around on the seat. "I don't mean to pry, but being a private eye—what's it really like? Why do you do it? I keep thinking of Bogart."

There were so many ways to answer her. The you-don't-know-the-troubles-I've-seen-sister version: world-weary and wise. The hard case: cynical but with a soft spot. A two-legged Tootsie Roll pop. The last romantic: burnt out and needing the redemption of a good woman. The masked avenger: the .45 caliber messiah. I decided to play it straight—for her big eyes, her wide mouth and the empty place in my chest.

"I've changed my answer to that a lot over the years. I once thought I did it just so I could help people. I don't believe that anymore, or rather that's only a part of it. I really don't have a very clear answer these days. I only know I'm obsessed with loss. Maybe I'm trying to inoculate myself against it. You know, get cowpox to avoid smallpox. I don't know." I flicked my eyes at her. She was looking at me intently. Maybe she cared about the answer.

"Have you ever lost anything yourself?"

"Good question. I'm not sure I've ever lost anything important. I don't know why it's so damned important to me. Believe me, I've chased myself around on this one like a dog with mange. With about the same degree of success. "How did you get into writing?" I tried not to sound too abrupt in moving away from myself as a topic.

"Bloodlines, partly. Habit. Not knowing or wanting to do anything else. All of the above. My father's an English professor and an unpublished novelist. That's part of it. I began to write stories when I was seven. I also used to tell stories to my little brother to help him get to sleep. Our mother died when I was twelve and he was six. He had nightmares a lot and trouble sleeping. Anyway, I had the usual tortured adolescent diary phase. I went off to college, majored in English and kept writing stories for my locked desk drawer. My best friend sent two of them to the school literary magazine. I could have killed her. They were accepted. I thought about graduate school, either a creative writing program or an advanced degree in English Lit. so I could teach. Anyway, to make a long story short, I did neither. I got a job waitressing and kept fiddling with writing stories. One day I read a novel that was so badly written I couldn't believe it. I said, 'I can write better than that.' It was put up or shut up time. I polished up some stories and submitted them. They were accepted, and I've been at it ever since. So far, it's paid all my bills and lets me keep at it. That's all I want right now."

"Well, I'll be very interested in reading your book." There was a pause as our verbal gropings skidded to a halt. Fortunately, we were near the exit I had been looking for.

We had gotten off at Georgia Avenue and gone down into Silver Spring. Crisfield's is a hole in the wall near the railroad overpass. It's also the best place to eat seafood in Washington. The line on Fridays is insane: they take no reservations and every good Catholic in Maryland is there.

The floor is black-and-white tile, the walls hospital green. For many years shelves of antique beer steins hung on the walls. They were destined one day for the Smithsonian should it outlive Crisfield's. Burglars stole them a couple of years ago. The police think a German collector financed the heist. The kitchen respects the bay and its creatures. Uncut by breadcrumbs or fillers and unperfumed with fancy seasonings, they're allowed to speak for themselves. The place has won enough dining awards to sate a dozen downtown chefs. Crisfield's will probably go on unchanged as long as the bay does. That worries me.

We were early and went right into the dining room and seated ourselves. Our waitress appeared with menus in hand and recited the daily specials: soft shells, shad roe, fresh rockfish with backfin stuffing. She left us with the menus. I decided on a dozen cherrystones, the mixed seafood Norfolk and a draft. I looked up at Samantha.

"I think I'll have the chowder, the soft shells, and a draft," she announced.

Our waitress returned and took our order.

Samantha looked at me and said, "I'd like to play racquetball with you again. It was fun. I think we're pretty evenly matched too."

I met her gaze. "Seemed like it. I enjoyed it too, but frankly my knees can't take it."

She furrowed her brow. "Oh? What's the matter with them?"

"An old college injury."

"That's too bad," she said.

"Maybe we'll see each other in the weight room." Believe it.

Our dinners arrived, and she turned out to be as businesslike an eater as I am. Between mouthfuls we talked. Exchanging facts and figures, years and degrees, siblings and forebears, locations and durations. The outlines for a pair of lives. Details to follow. Perhaps. For now it was enough. I stretched back and watched her pick at the remains of a crab.

"Shall we go?"

She nodded and we got up, left a tip, and settled up on the way out.

The drive back was silent, and I could feel tension spring up between us. "Where do you live?"

"Alexandria. Beauregard and Duke."

We parked near the entrance to her building. I turned to look at her and found myself impaled between desire and deed. I searched her eyes. A silent signal passed between us. A widened iris perhaps. And that was that.

I looked down at her. "Can I see you again?"

"Sure. I had a nice time." With that she slid out of the car, pirouetted and was gone into her building. I watched her all the way in and then turned on the engine. I whistled all the way home.

When I arrived, I called my service. There was one message: A Mr. Benson called. Please call back ASAP. Fuck him. Not tonight.

Chapter 3

IN THE MORNING I GOT UP AND SPENT THIRTY MINUTES ON MY rowing machine. Then I showered and dressed. After I had eaten, I called my answering service. There was still only one message. A Mr. Benson had called and asked me to please call him back.

I sat at my kitchen table and dialed his number.

"Hello."

"Mr. Benson, this is Leo Haggerty returning your call."

"Yes, uh, I've reconsidered and, uh, we'd like to hire you." Each word seemed to be dragged up out of his throat like coal from a played out mine and dumped a lump at a time into the phone.

I wondered what had gone into his new decision? Had his wife upped the ante? Was he realizing he was in over his head? "All right. I'll be out to see you in a half hour." I was about to hang up the phone when Benson began again.

"Uh, listen, I want you to work on this case on one condition. You're to keep me informed of everything you find out. I don't want you out there doing anything to endanger my baby. Do you understand? And there's no need to involve my wife in this. She's not well, and there's no need to upset her any more than Randi already has."

What the hell is going on, I wondered. Not only does he want in, now he's cut his wife out. Nobody wants me talking to the other one, that's for sure. "Mr. Benson, like I said, I'll see you in a half hour."

Round two at Belle Haven. I rang the door bell and admired the carvings on the door. Then it was yanked open and filled by Mr. Benson. We stared at each other for a moment. An undercurrent of dislike had drowned civility.

"May I come in?"

"Yeah—yes, I'm sorry. Come on in."

I headed back to the living room, wondering where Mrs. Benson was. Benson spoke to my back, inviting me to take a seat and asking me if I wanted a drink. I said no and sat on the sofa. He headed to the bar and made himself a drink. I decided to start from my end this time, not his.

"Let's get the ground rules clear. I charge two hundred and fifty dollars a day plus expenses; you get an itemized bill on completion. Routine items I expect carte blanche, extraordinary ones I'll check with you first. If you want references I can give you the names of police officers, attorneys, or other clients. If you're square with me up front I'll do everything I can to help you, including telling you not to hire me. If you lie to me all bets are off. I also require the daily rate up front. Expenses I get at the end of a job. We sign a contract for X number of days on the job." I sat back waiting to see what he'd do with all that.

"All right, fine. I want you to find my daughter and return her to me. I want to be kept informed of your actions." He hadn't even taken a deep breath to think about my conditions. Either they didn't bother him or he figured all along to break them, whatever they were going to be.

"One more thing. On missing child cases, I work two ways. One, I do all the work. The other way, you take off some time and go with me to help find her. Sometimes it means something to the kids knowing that a parent went looking for them. They aren't so eager to take off again. Also, I charge less that way."

Benson waved the offer away. "The money doesn't mean anything to me. You do it."

"Okay. You'll get a telephone report daily and a written one on completion." I hesitated a second. "Why haven't you called the police?"

"The police! That's a laugh. They couldn't find their asses with both hands and a map. No, they'd just give her description to the scout cars and that's it. They'd have to run her over to find her that way. Believe me, I've been looking. She's gone to ground somewhere. I want a pro on the job and on this job only." He bit off his sentence and dropped some ice cubes into his drink.

When he returned I started up again. "How did you get my name?"

He looked me straight in the face and sniggered. "I didn't. My wife dug you up, remember." I checked to see if I had fallen off the evolutionary ladder. "Where from I don't know. When I decided to hire you I called my attorney. He said you were the one that popped the lid on the Saunders case. So I figured I'd give you a shot at this."

"I'll need a current photo of your daughter, a list of her friends, and a letter introducing me as your agent. While you're doing that I'd like to look in her room to get a feeling for what kind of kid she is. Which room is hers?"

He pointed down the hall to the last door on the left and said he'd make up the list and the letter.

I went down to the door and stopped a moment, trying to clear my head, to be fresh for my first encounter with Miranda Benson. Her room would tell me something of who she was and what kind of world she lived in. If my head was clear I might be able to see the strands of wish and need that would propel her. From those I might get an inkling of her route and destination.

I took a deep breath, focused on the blank wall and stood there until my head was cleared. Then I entered her room.

The curtains and covers were pink and frilly. There was a dainty girl's desk and an ornate girl's bed, but that was all stuff her parents probably bought. There were no personal touches or flourishes; no wall full of rock star posters, no bed full of stuffed toys. I hate tossing kid's rooms. The secrets were always the same and I shouldn't be the first to know them.

I went to the desk and opened each drawer. The top one was full of school supplies. I leafed through some note pads full of geometric doodles. A series of ever darker rectangles, each getting smaller leading to a black center. A series of rectangles moving from black to yellow then back to a black center. Nothing else on the pages. The bottom two drawers were empty. I took out the drawers looking for any taped secrets; pictures, letters or a diary. I came up with nothing. I looked at her bookcase. A lot of old Newbery and Caldecott winners. I wondered who chose them. Lots of albums, alphabetically ordered and spanning the spectrum. I moved the bookcase away from the wall. Then I flipped through the most used books. Zippo. I moved the rug and the bed. I went to her dresser. The top drawers were full of rumpled jeans and tops. Some cotton shirts, long sleeve, and some similar denims. At the bottom was a black stretch tank top with EAT YOUR HEART OUT written across the bust in sequins. The next drawer was underwear, night-gowns, bras, a bikini, and tampons. The bottom drawer had some sweaters and a cheerleader's outfit. They were all folded, crisp, clean and looked untouched. I took the drawers out. Nothing. I crossed to the closet. Dresses, skirts, cotton pants— also all folded, clean and untouched. Boots and heels on the far side. I bent down and touched them for dust and came up positive. On the near side well-worn Nikes and a pair of sandals. I sensed someone behind me and turned my head to see who it was. She had red toenails and dimpled knees. She was cute, wide-eyed, and serious. She was about seven.

"Hello. What's your name?"

"Tammy."

"Well, my name's Leo. Pleased to meet you." I got up off my knees, dusted off my pants and held out my hand to her. She slipped her tiny hand into mine. I sat down on the bed to be more on her level.

"You're Randi's sister, right?" She nodded yes.

"Do you have any other brothers or sisters?" No. "Do you know where your sister is?"

"She's on a field trip. The other kids go on them sometimes at school." I nodded understanding. A field trip for sure. Into the human zoo. A crazy place, only the predators are uncaged. I thought about how to ask her about her family.

"Find anything?" Benson was in the doorway, holding some papers. Before I could answer he snapped at his daughter. "Tammy, why don't you go out and play?" She winced briefly, said, "Okay, Daddy," and slipped out of the room.

I went back to searching the room. I threw off the covers and moved the mattress. Then the springs, then the frame. I replaced the set of headphones that were hooked up to her stereo. I moved the bed back and saw a night light sticking out of a socket by the bed. I sat back on the bed wondering at that.

"No, nothing, just getting a sense of her. Has she changed her room in any way recently?"

"Yeah, she gave away her toys. Took down her posters. She let it all go to pot, always a mess."

"How about her clothes?"

"She stopped wearing the clothes we bought her. It was always painter's pants and big work shirts. Christ, she looked like a boy, buried in all that stuff. Anyway, here's the stuff you wanted. Last year's picture, the last friends she told us anything about and the authorization letter." He handed them to me.

"Did she have a teacher or counselor she was close to or might have talked to?"

"*No,*" he said, as he scanned an internal tape. "Well, maybe Miss Simpson; she was her phys ed teacher and cheerleader coach."

I added her name to the list and read the letter. "Who was her best friend, oldest and closest?"

"The Bradley girl. They just live down the block."

I looked finally at the picture, a typical head and shoulders shot. She had blonde hair, layered short in front and long in back. Her eyebrows were darker, full and arched strongly across her face, emphasizing her pale blue eyes. Her nose was upturned and her full lower lip pouted out. Her chin was squared off, strong and dimpled. "How different does she look these days?"

"Her hair is straight, long, over her shoulders. She doesn't take care of it. She's lost some weight, living on junk food. You can see it in her face. Her cheeks are hollowed out."

I looked at the picture and mentally modified it. I'd get a copy made and have an artist draw in the changes. "How big is she, and what was she wearing when she went to school Friday?"

"She's about five foot three and ninety-five to one hundred pounds. She was wearing what she always wears: white painter's pants, a blue long-sleeve work shirt and her Nikes."

I pulled out a contract from my coat pocket and suggested to Mr. Benson we return to the living room. I wrote out the particulars and handed it to him. He skimmed it, signed it and went to another room. He returned with a check for seven hundred and fifty dollars. I pocketed it and told him he'd hear from me this evening. I was going to start with Becky Bradley today and try to get the teacher tomorrow at school. Benson was at the table staring into space when I let myself out. No one was home at the Bradley house when I stopped by. I decided to go over to the Route 1 corridor and grab a bite to eat.

Fairfax County is one of the richest counties in America, and the Route 1 corridor is a ten-mile slash through it of fast food places, gas stations, trailer parks, and hot sheet motels. You can eat and go, gas and go, pick up your home and go, fuck and go. At the south end there's a combat zone around Fort Belvoir of massage parlors, topless bars, and adult book stores.

No one lives on Route 1. Everybody's just passing through no matter how long they stay. Olde Towne or Belle Haven is where they want to be. Every day you can get up and watch your neighbors a half mile on either side of the corridor living out your dreams. Far too often down here that sight ends in the late night shattering of glass, the thunderclap of gunfire and a police siren's whiny song.

I pulled into the Dixie Pig's lot, parked, and walked across to the front doors. The Dixie Pig is one of a handful of places on the corridor where they take more time to cook your food than you took to order it. It's a landmark on Route 1, fifty years in one place. Entering it is like entering a time warp. The prices are from 1952 and so are the waitresses. In their beehive hairdos and starched whites, they call you honey and offer to sit on your lap as if they were eighteen and their daughters weren't. The barbecue is hot, juicy, shredded pork on a homemade bun with tangy slaw. I ordered a sandwich and a beer. When the sandwich arrived I doused it with jalopeño vinegar. I ate and headed back to the Bradley house.

Chapter 4

THE BRADLEYS WERE THREE HOUSES DOWN FROM THE BENSONS. I pulled into the driveway in front of a similar colonial mansion. I got out and went to the front door. There was a knocker shaped like an Aztec sun medallion. It boomed off the solid wood door. A petite oriental woman appeared. I took a stab, "Mrs. Bradley?"

"Yes, I am Mrs. Bradley."

"My name is Leo Haggerty. I'm a private investigator looking for Miranda Benson. I understood your daughter had been a friend of hers. I'd like to speak to her if I could."

She began to pull back into the house. I withdrew my wallet, flipped open to my ID card and extended it to her. She took it and read it carefully, glancing up to match the photo to my face. She handed it back. As she did I handed her the letter of authorization from Benson. Reading that seemed to do it.

"Becky is at the club right now. She has a swimming meet. I'm going over there now. You can follow me and talk to her there." She turned away from the door and picked up a purse.

I stepped away from her and followed her down to the driveway. She got into a powder-blue Mercedes. I got into my car and backed it out into the street. She followed suit and we headed down to Potomac Shores Country Club. We went up through the entrance gates around past the porte cochere to a lot just past the clubhouse. I followed her to the clubhouse, then through the lobby. She turned and motioned to a door and told me it was to the men's locker room and that it was the shortest route to the pool. I went in, weaving through a slalom of towel clad men, talking about birdies and pars, knockers and jugs. I stepped outside and looked for Mrs. Bradley. She came up to me and pointed to her daughter.

"That's Becky. I'd appreciate it if you'd wait until after her race. She's anxious enough about this as it is."

I nodded assent and looked at her daughter. Her mother's almond eyes were set in a narrow face. She had straight black hair that she was wearing in a long braid. She coiled it on top of her head and pulled her cap on over it. In the battle between hydrodynamics and boy appeal, boy appeal was winning. She was all limbs and joints in her blue Speedo suit. Her race was called, girls thirteen to fifteen, fifty meters freestyle. She stepped up to the pool and ran a finger around the bottom of her suit, snapping it in place. She shook out her arms and legs the way a wet dog does, then went into her starting crouch.

I looked back at her mother, who was leaning forward in her chair, mouth set, wound up with her daughter's tension. The starting pistol cracked and six girls hit the water. Becky was quick off the mark and had a slight lead at fifteen meters. I wondered how her turn was. In a fifty it can make or break you, regardless of what you do before and after. She hit the wall a half body in front and came out well, a good push and just at the surface. In the far lane a big girl had been gaining on her for the last twenty meters. At forty, strength and stamina began to count. Becky was holding on but that was it—no kick. The girl in the far lane was attacking the water, pulling through it as if it were sand. At forty-five she caught Becky and at the wall she had her.

Becky had her arms over the edge of the pool, sucking in wind. She looked up at the announcer for the results and set her face for an instant when she found out she was second. Her mother had relaxed and was breathing through her mouth. She looked at me and said, "Let me talk to her for a minute, then I'll bring her over. Do you want to talk with her alone?"

"Yes. I'd appreciate that very much."

She walked over and picked up a towel from a pool-side table and draped it over her daughter. They put their heads together and talked briefly. Becky turned and glanced at me then back at her mother. She huddled in the towel and dried herself off. She pulled off her cap and unwound her hair. She looked at me again for a moment and came my way.

I stood up and motioned for her to sit. She did and looked at me intently. "My name is Leo Haggerty. I'm a private investigator and I'd like to talk to you about Miranda Benson. I understand you were friends." I pulled out my wallet and held my ID out to her. She took it, matched face and photo and returned it.

"Why do you want to talk to me? Why don't you just ask Randi?"

"I can't. It appears Randi ran away from home and I'm trying to help her parents find her. Can you help me? I was told you and she were close for a while, then drifted apart. Can you tell me why?"

She looked steadily at me for a moment, trying to read me for a sign of what to do. Perhaps I've a kindly face. I doubt it. Most likely her parents were not yet her adversaries and her mother told her it was okay to talk to me, so she talked to me.

"Randi and I were pretty good friends until this year. We were cheerleaders and were on the school newspaper. We had the same homeroom and classes together. I don't know what happened. She just weirded out, you know?"

"No. What do you mean 'weirded out'?"

"She just dropped our whole crowd. She stopped going to lunch with us. We didn't do homework together or sit together in classes anymore. She stopped going to parties or coming over to my house. Then she quit cheerleaders and the newspaper. She was angry all the time, saying everything was garbage and things like that. She just sat in class doing nothing or just skipped and hung out in the halls. One day after school was over, I saw her in the bathroom. I wanted, you know, to see if we could still be friends. She started crying real hard and I asked her what was the matter. She said, 'We can't be friends, we just can't. Don't you know that?' I asked her why, and she just blew up and said to leave her alone and walked out. Pretty soon she was hanging out with Angie and Cindy and the rest of the mall rats."

"Mall rats?"

"Yeah, the freaks and grits that hang out all the time at the mall."

The shift from genus to species hadn't made things a whole lot clearer.

"Did you notice anything going on between her and her parents while this was happening?"

"They were just really angry with each other all the time. Her father used to come and pick her up from school every day and used to really ask her a lot of questions about what she was doing."

"What do you think was going on with Randi?" I noticed she was starting to squirm in her seat and look away from me. I could feel her cooperation coming to an end, and she was closing me out fast. "Can you tell me the names of those two girls again?"

"Angie Martindale and Cindy Fosburg."

"Do they live in Belle Haven?"

"No, they live in Bucknell. Uh, I have to be going now, okay?"

"Yeah. Thanks very much; you've been very helpful. Good luck in your next meet. Would you tell your mother I'll find my way out and tell her thanks also?" She said yes and headed back to her friends and family.

I went back out through the grill room, found the lobby and left through the front door.

I stood on the portico, my eyes shaded from the sun by the awning and tried to bring Randi Benson to life. An angry and hurt girl who had changed in some way, that was what people kept saying.

Chapter 5

I TURNED AROUND AND WALKED BACK INTO THE LOBBY AND ASKED the receptionist where the phones were. She pointed to a pay phone in a corner and I went to it. I sat on the bench and flipped through the phone book for Fosburg and Martindale. I was in luck—only one of each in this area. I wrote down the addresses and headed back to my car.

Bucknell was a middling neighborhood. People here were working and making it, but barely. The desperation was quieter here than on Route 1; they still had something to lose. Bucknell sat below the hills of Belle Haven and Belle View and inland from Arcturus and the Potomac palaces. Money finds its way up hills and down to the shore. The poor get what's left. I turned onto Quander Road and began looking for Angie Martindale's home. I pulled up in front of it and left the car running for a second. It was a square two story wood frame house. Inside it was dark and without curtains. The lawn was unmowed and full of weeds. Paint was peeling on the side walls. I could see a clothes tree in the backyard. A beat-up white Fairlane sat in the driveway. I cut off the engine and headed to the house. I glanced at the car as I went by. The bumper sticker asked me to honk if I loved Jesus. There were two empty Schlitz Lights on the back seat and a pair of foam dice draped over the rearview mirror.

I stepped up to the front door, opened the screen and knocked. No answer. I waited a couple of seconds and knocked again louder. This time there was movement inside. The door came open and a woman in a housecoat appeared. She hugged herself and rocked to her own music. There were curlers in her streaked blonde hair. A cigarette was stuck between her fingers

23

and on her feet were pale blue slippers with fluffy balls on top. Her face was all knobs and slashes. Her eyes were dark and empty like the windows in a bombed building. She looked as if life had steamrolled her flat and when she came out from under the rollers all she had left was amazement that she was alive. What to do with that life was beyond her. She eyed me with the half crafty look of someone searching for an escape hatch, not a chance to turn the tables. Once you get that look, your life isn't your own. It belongs to any predator who can find you. She eyed me head to toe. I don't think it mattered who I was. I wanted to bleed her, that's all she saw.

"Is this the Martindale residence and is Angie home? I'd like to speak with her."

"No, she ain't home and what do you want with her?" She tried to snarl but it came out half whimper.

"I understand she knows Randi Benson. I'm looking for her. She's run away."

"I don't know anything about that. She don't tell me about her friends. She knows everything." She started to pull back and close the door.

"Uh, Mrs. Martindale, do you know where Angie is now?"

"No. She's probably at the mall. They all hang out at the mall or at some friend's. I don't know." She waved her hand as if accounting for her daughter was a winged buzzing nuisance she wanted to brush off and me with it. When I didn't move she glared at me. "She's a big girl now, at least she sure as hell thinks she is. When I was her age I was on my own. She may as well learn how. I ain't gonna take care of her." The door slammed and she was gone.

I backed off the step and let the screen swing slowly, gently closed. I got in my car and checked on the Fosburg address. It was two blocks down. I pulled up and got out. The house and yard were similar. I went to the door and knocked and knocked and knocked. Nothing. I returned to my car and thought about going to the mall, but I had no idea what Angie or Cindy looked like. I didn't want to go around asking everybody if they'd seen so-and-so. They'd be gone if they heard some strange adult was asking about them. Randi hadn't had a yearbook in her room. I'd get that tomorrow at school when I saw her teacher Miss Simpson. For now, I'd go visit an artist I knew to update the picture of Randi Benson and then grab some dinner.

Josh Walters did freelance art and photo work for ad agencies. I rang his apartment door bell and waited. In a couple of seconds I heard Josh come to the door. "Who is it?"

"Josh, it's me, Leo Haggerty. I've got some rush work."

"All right, Leo. Come in." He swung the door open and bowing a little, waved me in. Josh is tiny, 5′3″ or so, sharp featured with pale freckled skin and red hair he combs up from the back so that it sits like a wreath around his head.

"What've you got for me, Leo?"

"A photo, a year old. I want you to change it to make it look current, then make me four copies, okay?"

He nodded. "Sure. Show it to me."

I dug it out of my pocket and handed to him.

"Pretty thing. How do you want it changed?" he asked.

"Her hair is now straight, long and not well cared for. She's lost some weight, jawline's sharper. Cheeks hollowed out, eyes probably have shadows around them."

"All right, Leo. When do you need them?" He was looking deeply at the photo, doing the work in his mind.

"Pronto, old buddy. When can you have them for me?"

"Tomorrow morning. How's that?"

"Fine. I'll pick them up. Noon okay? And clip a bill to it."

He nodded and we shook hands. Josh headed to his easel and I let myself out.

When I got back to my house I sat at the desk, emptying my pockets. I dug out a manila folder and put a number on the tab. Into it went my contract with Benson. I pulled paper out of the desk, rolled it into the typewriter and punched out my report. I Xeroxed a copy of it and stuck it in the folder with the original. I cleared my service. No client calls.

I went through my mail. It was the usual mix of magazines,

bills and garbage. Except there was a letter from Wendy Sullivan. Actually, it was just a note clipped to a recent *Track World* photograph of her. I held the picture up and stared at it. It was a good shot, much as I remembered her in one of her happier moments that week we spent together last year when we were both on the mend.

Her note said she'd thrown the javelin sixty-seven meters at the Golden Gate Invitational and was closing in on the U.S. record. She'd also just finished training to be a companion in the university victim assistance program "for all the unearned kindness I've known." Her note also said she missed me. I left the note and the picture on the desk. I missed her too.

I kicked off my shoes and went to the kitchen. Squatting in front of the refrigerator I waited for a volunteer to say "eat me." No one showed up. I went back to my office and called Benson.

His wife picked up the phone. I asked to speak to her husband.

She held the phone a second and then said, "So he got to you too." Her voice was the hybrid offspring of a sneer and a whine.

I thought frost was forming on my receiver. "Mrs. Benson, I couldn't be your agent if you weren't going to acknowledge hiring me. This is not secret agent stuff. I like working in the sunlight with my eyes open. Your husband hired me and he's willing to play by some of my rules. The end result is the same— I'm going to find your daughter." I waited to see what she'd say.

"I quite doubt that." She and her husband were too busy cutting each other down to see anything as a common interest.

After a minute Benson picked up the phone. "Yes, Haggerty. What have you got?"

I ran through my day for him and my plans for tomorrow. He punctuated my report with grunts. The rhinoceros returned in my mind. He was on his hind legs with a phone in one hand and a drink in the other. I told him I'd call him tomorrow if anything broke. I put down the phone and checked my watch. It was almost five. I went back to the kitchen. Nothing looked very appealing. Rather, cooking for myself wasn't too appealing.

Maybe I'd go out to eat or just not eat. I got a Guinness from the refrigerator, opened it and began to meander through the house. I looked at my office: my files, my books, my trophies. I wandered out to the living room and looked at my albums. I had an itch that I couldn't scratch. But I could name it, I bet. I bent over and tried to find a record to play, but I couldn't concentrate at all. Everytime I tried to set up a thought and relate it to others, it disappeared. It was like trying to play chess in a wind tunnel. I got up and walked out to the glass doors and looked across the lawn. Everything was quiet. I looked back into the house. I had everything I wanted, just the way I liked. It wasn't enough. Samantha's face kept floating up before me. Maybe I was rushing things? No, I was getting too old to be coy. Carpe diem. I picked up the phone.

It rang four times. Then, "Hello?"

"Samantha, this is Leo Haggerty. I was wondering if you were doing anything tonight?"

"Yeah. I'm going to soak my brain to undo all the damage from the library. I think I've fused all my synapses."

"Can I interest you in going dancing? It's very therapeutic." I was held there dangling on the question's hook. I dangled a good long while.

"Okay, I guess. Let me bathe and change. Why don't I drive over and meet you at your place?"

I gave her directions from Alexandria via Route 7.

"See you in, say, an hour and a half."

"Fine."

"Bye." I could feel her presence slipping down the black coiled wire and the old chill of loneliness fill me up. Before Wendy Sullivan I didn't notice it. Maybe I hadn't known what it was until then. These days it seemed to be there more and more often.

Chapter 6

I PULLED OUT THE POWERS GOLD LABEL AND POURED AN INCH into a tumbler. I put R.E.M. on the turntable, slid into my recliner and angled it toward the patio door. The Irish went down my throat as smoothly as the sun slid below the horizon. I thought about Wendy Sullivan. Apart from some phone calls at first and now some notes, I hadn't been in touch with her since the trial almost eight months ago. She held up pretty well through that experience. I sat right behind her in the courthouse and when things got bad I slid my hands through the balustrade that separated us and held her hand. Nights we walked and talked on the beach. She was healing slowly. She slept well most nights, went shopping by herself now and hadn't had a panic attack in six weeks. The night the trial ended we went dancing. Dancing with her highlighted all of the tensions in our relationship: holding her hand in my hand, my arm around her waist, her face so close to mine. I remembered the bright blue eyes, the long gentle slope of her neck when her head tilted back to laugh, the rich exuberance of that sound. For a while I had been able to file Wendy under "victim," but when I no longer saw her that way my sexual feelings for her emerged anew. I told myself that it was the age difference that kept me from pursuing her. That was rational and it was true. It was also a balm I applied when it became clear she didn't feel the same toward me. So I packed and patted my sexual feelings into a small hard ball, closed my eyes and threw it as far away as I could. I'd never been just a friend to a woman I desired. It was time I started to learn how to do that. So friends we became.

I sipped some more of the whiskey and listened to a couple of other LPs. The door bell rang. I went to answer it. Through the peephole I got an eyeful. She had on a black felt fedora tipped low over one eye, large white earrings, a white silk blouse open at the throat, black silk pants and slingback heels. I unlocked the deadbolt and let her in.

"You ready to go?" she asked. I wondered who was taking whom.

"Yeah. Just let me lock up." I went through the house turning out the lights, locked the patio doors, made sure the stereo was off and followed her out the front door. I pulled the door closed, locked the deadbolt and activated the alarm system.

"Why an alarm system?"

"My office is in the house. I keep all my case files here. The things in those files are nobody's business but mine and my clients'."

We walked down the driveway. I slowed at the door to my car. Samantha said, "How about I drive?" I shrugged and followed her to an old red Mustang. Samantha got in and I walked around the car as she reached across the front seat and pulled up the door lock. When I got in she asked where we were going.

"The Fountain of Youth. It's out Route 7, past Tyson's Corner, on the same side of the road as Clyde's."

"Okay."

She swung around the court and turned right on Gallows Road. A left turn on to Route 7 took us past Bloomingdale's and the rest of the concrete metastases that were Tyson's Corner. We went past Clyde's. Just before Route 7 became the Leesburg Pike I pointed out the bar on the right. Samantha turned and pulled into the lot. We got out and walked across to the entrance. Coming here alone was an act of desperation. At the bar people careened into each other like it was a demolition derby. Hi, my name's Garth, you into sportfucking? The dance floor was a peaceful respite from that. They played songs you could dance to, really dance to. Here the idea was that you had a partner you were dancing with, not at. Not too long ago I'd followed some kids into a slam-dancing bar downtown and came out worse off than at a couple of professional beatings I'd been invited to.

Samantha and I went in and looked for a table with a pair of adjoining empty stools. I saw one, took her hand and led her toward it. We slid onto the stools and caught the waitress's eye. She came over to us.

"What would you like?"

I nodded to Samantha. "Bourbon and soda on the rocks."

"Irish whiskey, neat," I said.

We swiveled around on our stools to see the dance floor. The place wasn't packed yet. After a drink we'd get out on the floor. I asked her how her day went.

"Not too bad. Doing research is the least fun part of writing."

"What were you looking up?"

"Just some of the new advances in care for premature infants. I'm writing a story about a rural couple whose premature baby is flown into a major medical center—like Fairfax Hospital's intensive care nursery—and how the couple copes with the hi-tech efforts to save the baby while they're trying to connect with the child themselves. Did you know that some parents, mothers usually, have a psychotic episode after all that and show up weeks later at the hospital to return the baby saying that it isn't theirs?"

"Jesus, what a start in life."

She stopped for a second, then said, "How about your day?"

"Pretty typical. Missing child case. Seems like a lousy home situation. I'll find her pretty soon and take her back. Three months from now she'll bolt again. I ought to install beepers in the kids I find. Make finding them again easier."

"Sounds pretty depressing to me."

"Yeah. I guess so. You keep a lid on it. Otherwise it'll eat you up."

"I don't think I could do work like that. Writing about things like that is as close as I want to get."

"If I only thought about the outcomes it'd get to me too. But each case is a fresh start. Sometimes things do turn out okay.

When they don't I just try to focus on whether I did the best I could. You can't take a client's troubles on as your own. That's the express lane to the rubber room."

Our drinks came. I raised my glass to toast her. Unfortunately for this encounter, my wit was missing in action. "Enough talk of bad endings. To beautiful beginnings."

She nodded her acceptance of that toast and we touched glasses.

"Shall we dance?" I held out my hand to her.

"Love to." She slipped her hand into mine and we walked out to the dance floor. I put my arm around her waist. She laid her hand on my shoulder. We began to move together: surprisingly pleasantly, fluidly. Wendy Sullivan taught me to dance. Rather she taught me not to be so self-conscious that I wouldn't try.

On the faster songs our dancing was restrained. No pelvic thrusts, no shaking fannies, no bump and grind, no frantic melting into the beast with two backs. The intensity was all in our eyes. Every so often I felt us exchange frank appraisals of what might be with no attempt to make it happen.

Slowly over the next couple of hours her hand came to rest on the back of my neck, our cheeks would brush, our temples touch, and I held her hand against my chest. Eventually, it was closing time and we meandered out of the bar, hand in hand, listing a bit against each other. How much of that was affection and how much alcohol I didn't know.

When we arrived at my house Samantha asked to use the bathroom. I opened the front door and let us in. I pointed down the hall to our left. "Bathroom's the first door on the left, opposite my office."

As she walked down the hall I wondered what she thought of what she saw. As surely as Randi Benson's personality was reflected in her room so did my self speak out from these walls. I knew what aspects of myself I wanted the world to see. What else was revealed I did not know. She came out of the bathroom and stood in the doorway looking at the living and dining rooms.

Again I wondered what she saw. I wondered if she saw a space with her name on it.

"Can I have the nickel tour?"

"Sure." I crossed over to her and pointed to the room on her right. "This is my office." She stepped in and flicked on the light. There was a bookcase on one wall. She went to it and began fingering the spines of books.

"You read funny things. I mean I guess I didn't expect you to read these kinds of books. It's all novels and some philosophy. I guess I expected legal codes and technical stuff."

"These tell me more about people than all the legal cases ever written."

She continued to look at my books. "Do you know that you don't have a single novel written by a woman? I'm not sure I could send my 'baby' into such a forbidding place."

I threw up my hands and tried for a contrite smile. "I'm ready to mend my ways. How shall I begin?"

"I'll get a few books together for you. Some Anne Tyler, Margaret Atwood, Jayne Anne Phillips. There's a whole 'nother world out there."

Tell me about it. Please.

She turned to my desk with the typewriter, telephone and draftsman's lamp. My license was framed above it. Next to that were my locked files and in one corner my locked gun case. The other corner had my easy chair, side table and reading light.

She turned slowly and looked at me. "Tell me something. Are you carrying a gun?"

I turned around and lifted up my coattails. She saw the butt of my Bren 10 sticking out above my waist band.

She shook her head. "Jesus Christ. I'm going out with a guy who carries a gun. Guns scare me. People who carry guns scare me."

There was nothing I could say. Sometimes I was scared for me and sometimes scared of me. I'd walked away from a lot of dangerous situations. I'd also gone looking for a few.

I was starting to get uncomfortable with this and pointed

toward the bedroom. "The bathroom you've seen; this is the bedroom."

She stuck her head in and looked around. I told her the shower was around the corner. When she turned toward me our eyes met again as they had a couple of times on the dance floor. For a moment we just looked at each other. Swiftly my orbit began to decay and I started my descent. I kissed her. Then she kissed me. We were fitting our mouths together as if to heal a common wound. For a moment our tongues danced like snakes and our arms wound around each other. Abruptly, we parted.

I pulled her body close to me. She gently pushed her fists against my chest. I released her.

"No more. Not now. I'm tired of being modern. I'm not saving it for marriage or anything. It's just I stopped liking myself when I was giving it away all the time. I never seemed to get what I wanted in the deal so I'm cautious these days, that's all." She shrugged her shoulders. "Look, I like you, okay. But I'm also a little afraid of you. You don't look like a safe bet to me. Before we go any further sexually I want to know a little more about what I'm getting into with you."

She smiled ruefully. "Sex is not dentistry, the slick filling of aches and cavities. Not for me anymore."

"I'll buy that. Is the line yours?"

"No. It's from one of those women writers I'm going to introduce you to: Margaret Atwood."

"Okay. So be it. I'm not just interested in you horizontally."

"That's nice to know." She brightened. "I think I'd better leave now. I've got a long day tomorrow."

"Okay."

She picked up her purse and went to the door. After letting her out I stood in the driveway and watched her pull away up the street. I waved good-bye but couldn't tell if she saw me.

Chapter 7

FIVE-THIRTY CAME AND I REACHED OVER AND CUFFED MY ALARM'S ears, trying to still the gonging in my head. I staggered up to my feet and quietly padded to the bathroom. My mouth felt like someone had turned over an ashtray in it. I gargled, brushed my teeth and rinsed my eyes. I'd shave at the club. Getting dressed, I thought of Samantha as I was slipping on my Bianchi shoulder holster. Would I ever become as comfortable with her as I was in it? I combed my hair and went to the kitchen.

I take my work seriously, and staying in good condition is essential. Might may not make right but it sure does make do. What quickness and agility I'd had was gone. They're gifts anyway. Strength and endurance you earn. You get to keep them only as long as you work for them. Whenever I can I try to work out.

Most days, that's with my associate Arnie Kendall in the weight room. Once a week we shoot at his range and then we hit the mats.

I got to the club, locked my car and went in. As I was signing in I looked up and saw Arnie coming toward me. He's the same size I am, about six feet tall, two hundred pounds. He looks like something you'd dream up in macramé class: all ropes and cables, knots and braids. He changes his appearance regularly. Sometimes he's bald, sometimes bearded, sometimes a Mohawk, sometimes a Vandyke. Today he was Fu Manchu, complete with topknot.

I've worked with Arnie enough times in enough tight places to know I can count on him to do what needs doing. In fact, I know very little about him except that he's very good at what he does. Courtesy of Green Beret University, Vietnam Campus.

I stuck out my hand to greet him. He enveloped it, pumped my arm and returned it.

"Ok! Let's get to it," I said.

"Fine."

We changed in the locker room and went up to the weight room. I passed my idol, "Captain Humble," on the way in. At sixty-six he can still bench press the Pentagon. I went through my stretching routine, then hit the weights. I worked on my lats, my pectorals, did my curls and dumbbell presses and then hit the bench. I did a set with 300 pounds to warm up my muscles and loosen the joints. Then I began to increase the weights: 350, 375, 400. Finally I put on a new maximum for myself: 425 pounds. I laid back on the bench and cinched my belt in another notch. I set my feet, twisting them onto the floor for the right feel. Arching my back, I wiggled on the bench, getting set. I looked at the plates and the bar, losing the world in their tiny irregularities. I set my shoulders and adjusted my grip, looking for the right feel in my fingers and palms. Arnie and Mo, the weight room coach, stood nearby to catch the bar. Benching without spotters is asking to die a painful death. If you can't manage the weight and it falls on your chest or across your throat, it's lights out. I began to pump my lungs, filling them and then settling into a rhythm. I mentally checked the feel of my feet, legs, back, grip. Then I began to empty my mind until only the pressure on my hands existed; when that had happened and my breathing was full and rhythmic I knew I was ready.

Lifting has the same stages as an orgasm: impending, inevitable, irreversible and then done. I bellowed and the bar began to rise. I could feel the shock down my forearms, through my shoulders and back. I was conscious of the pain and strain as my entire being was focused on moving over a fifth of a ton by millimeters. The reality of shattered joints, of tendons and muscles snapping off the bone like telephone lines in a tornado sat in the back of my mind. Fortunately, overwhelming pain is just that:

overwhelming. A brief flash and then shock. The mind just shuts down.

Finally, I made the lockout. Arnie and Mo helped guide the bar to the rack. My eyes focused on a hand reaching out to me. I shook it and sat up on the bench.

"Nice work. That's a new max." Arnie was smiling.

"Thanks."

I finished my workout with a couple of hundred sit-ups and a half-hour stretch on the rowing machine.

After showering Arnie and I went to sit in the sauna. While it was empty we talked.

"What're you doing these days, Leo?"

"Runaway kid—looks pretty easy at this point. Angry teenager. Home isn't what it ought to be. Maybe I'll find her staying at a girlfriend's house. I doubt it. More likely she's with a new boyfriend who, when he gets a load of her age, will drop her so fast she'll bounce for a week. Doesn't look like there's anything in it for you. There may be some surveillance if this really drags out but that's it." I pushed open the door and followed Arnie.

"That's cool. Listen, I've got the Colt fixed. I put on a slide release and a speed safety. While I was at it I put on new grips and combat sights and adjusted the trigger. I'll give it to you when we leave."

We showered and shaved and dressed quickly. On the street I followed Arnie to his car. He opened the trunk and unlocked the steel case. Inside were my Colt .45 in its pancake holster and a handgun I'd never seen before. He handed me my gun.

"What's that, Arnie?" I gestured to the case.

"That's a Grizzley .45 Magnum. I'm testing it for the shop. It's unreal. The thing'll stop a truck. The action is beautiful too, very smooth. They won't be on the market for a while. Here, heft it." He handed me the piece. It was a bit heavier than my Colt. A true hand cannon. I gave it back to Arnie and saw it disappear into his fist. He locked the trunk up again.

"Listen, I've got to hit the road. I'm going over to this kid's school. I'll see you Wednesday sometime. If this is cleared up by then we can go to the range. I'd like to try a few rounds with that thing—okay?"

"Sure. Good hunting." He folded himself into his car. I watched him back out and waved as he sped away.

I went by Samantha's apartment and caught 395 south to the beltway. Going east I stayed on the beltway past Route 1, then went south on the parkway. I preferred to use the parkway rather than Route 1 even if it wound up being the long way to some places. The school was off Fort Hunt Road below Bucknell and Belle Haven. I pulled into the driveway and up around the building to the visitor's lot. It was 8:45. I parked the car and headed to the main entrance. The school was one story, except for the gym in the background. Rows of slitted windows angled open. Trees and shrubs were planted right next to the building but nowhere else on the grounds.

I went into the school looking for the main office. The hall was filled with children and I stopped to watch them for a second. Examples of the current tribal groupings sauntered by: preps, freaks, punks, grits, and nerds. They all looked older than I remembered myself at that age. They seemed to be accelerating through childhood. Trying desperately to be adults even without all the equipment. The *g* forces of that pursuit twisted their features. The faster they went the more bent out of shape they got. I had wanted the same things at that age. It was just more furtive in my day. Whether that was a step up or a step back, I didn't know.

I went into the office and stood at the counter peering up and down to see if anyone would come to see me. After a couple of minutes a woman came out of the principal's office and asked if she could help me. She was short and had been starched, buttoned, cropped and pinched into a flat green skirt and white parochial school blouse. She wore a crucifix the size of a broadsword, flat black shoes and—I was sure—support hose.

"Yes. I'd like to speak with Miss Simpson, please."

"And who may I say is calling?" The words slipped out of her pinched mouth like air from a drowning man.

"Leo Haggerty."

She turned her back to me and went to one of the empty secretary's desks. After punching a few buttons and with her back still to me she spoke in a whisper. I wondered what I looked like to her. She covered the phone with her hands and turned back to me. "She wants to know what it is in regard to." Her back straightened just slightly. I wondered if she'd plant her feet soon and bar the door.

"It's a confidential matter. I'm a private investigator. I have a letter of authority from my client if she'd like to see that."

Again she huddled over the phone with her back to me. I leaned forward with my elbows on the counter, wondering when this would end. The last time females whispered in my presence I was fourteen and was making awkwardness an art form. If she started to giggle I was going to leave. She put down the phone and said, "Miss Simpson will be right down."

I turned to face the door. As I waited, leaning back on the counter, I wished I had a fedora to fondle or a cigarette to snarl around. Miss Simpson came briskly through the door. I thought someone had thrown snow down my shirt. She was an explosion in pastels: peaches and cream, golden blonde, pearly whites, baby blues. She wore white high-waisted slacks, sandals, a pink cotton blouse and plain gold jewelry. Hoops in her ears, a thin choker and bracelet and one ring. She reached out to shake my hand. My head was swirling with color shock. I was going to need goggles if she smiled again. Her hands were strong: small palms, short fingers and nails, no polish.

"I'd like to see that letter you mentioned, please." I reached into my coat for it and handed it to her. Her eyes zigzagged down the page and she folded it up and gave it back to me. Her mouth had set into a line and the light in her eyes was dimmed. She seemed to have set her body on "serious." "Come this way. We'll talk in my office." She spun on her toes like a marine honor guard doing about-face and I followed her out.

Her office was down by the gym. I followed her through the side marked Girls Gym. As she descended the stairs she said,

"The girls don't come in until after homeroom. There's no one down here." She opened her door and motioned me to a seat. I sat across from her in her painted cinder block office. She straightened papers on her gray steel desk. On top of a filing cabinet were a number of golden trophies of girls holding wreaths over their heads. I couldn't tell what sport they were for.

She looked up at me and said, "What do you want to know about Randi?"

"Everything and anything. I'm not sure what would be useful. She seemed like a kid who changed quite a bit in the last year—friends, interests, habits. I understand you were her phys ed teacher and cheerleader coach and probably knew her best of all her teachers."

"You're right. She did change quite a bit and I don't know why. She seemed at the start of the year to be a bright, eager kid who enjoyed school. She was pretty and popular." She stopped for a moment, perhaps trying to better fix Randi in her memory. "I guess the first thing to change was that she closed herself off. She didn't talk to anyone anymore. Then she dropped out of things. She dropped out of cheerleaders, dropped her friends and started cutting classes. Judging from her new friends I'd say it was a good bet that she was using some kind of drugs. Pot, Quaaludes, PCP, god only knows. I remember there were two strange incidents. One was the same week she quit cheerleaders. She was sitting in front of her locker, just staring. It was late, so I came by and told her to move it and get dressed. She really flared up and said she wouldn't, she wasn't coming to gym anymore. I asked her why but I couldn't get anything clear from her about what it was. She was a good athlete and she had an excellent body. Some girls are shy around the others if they don't feel as well developed so they come late to class and dress alone. But that couldn't have been it. Randi was popular with most girls and like I said a good athlete. Gym was kind of like a dessert for her. A treat compared to her other classes. She just refused to come back at all or even discuss it, even though she knew she'd get an *F* in the course. I don't know why she was so adamant."

"You mentioned there was another incident."

"Yes. Her father used to pick her up every day after practice. I mean, he was a hawk around that girl. He'd get her at the locker room door and walk her to the car. I remember once thinking that Randi looked like she was walking to the gallows or something when she went to that car. I don't know. Anyway what struck me as strange were Mr. Benson's questions the day she quit cheerleaders and left school. He sounded like he had no idea about her behavior changes at school. I was surprised. For someone who seemed so concerned about her he really didn't seem to know her very well at all." Her palms came down on the table to emphasize her point and end our time. She glanced at the clock for support and said, "Classes begin now so we'll have to stop. I hope this was helpful." I reached across the desk and we shook hands. Silence hung heavily between us. "And I hope you can find Randi and help her." I nodded my unspoken agreement and went back upstairs to the main floor.

Back at the school office I glanced at my watch and decided to call Josh from the phonebooth. He got the phone on the second ring. "Josh? Leo. Are the prints ready?"

"Yeah, Leo, no sweat. Strange looking kid; part child and part adult. Looks like she's in a time warp, aging faster than the rest of us."

"Listen, I'll be by to pick it up in about a half hour, okay?"

"Fine. See you then."

I went to my car figuring that I'd want to be at the mall around two-thirty to soak up the feel of the place and get settled in. I wanted to be part of the background the kids would come to populate. First I'd watch their migration patterns, social order and dominance rituals. Then I'd begin to move among them on my search. I realized in a flash that I didn't have pictures of either Angie Martindale or Cindy Fosburg. I went back into the school. On the bulletin board next to the office was a map of the school with a "you are here" mark to locate yourself. I found the library and walked down the hall toward it. There I met the librarian, who by her name tag was Mrs. Winchell. After letting her read Benson's letter I asked her for the current school yearbook. She gave it to me with a stare as if I were asking for pornography. I sat down at one of the tables and looked up the girls' names and the pages on which their pictures were. There were no group activity portraits, just the mug shots. I stared at them each a long time. This was going to be my one chance to memorize their looks. Angie Martindale: black hair with lots of curls, plucked eyebrows arched high like sooty rainbows over her eyes; button nose, a touch of baby fat still in her cheeks, small mouth with a bowed upper lip—a perennial pucker. Cindy Fosburg: brown hair straight down her back, long face not quite horsey—her features were better than that—straight nose, high broad forehead, prominent overbite so that her mouth was always partially open. She was barely prettier than a gopher. I etched them into my memory. Returning the book to Mrs. Winchell, I resisted my impulse to tell her that just as she'd thought there was a naked girl on page 47.

Josh's place was a half hour away. I rapped on the door and heard him cross the room. He let me enter, bowing with his arm sweeping an arc before him. "Enter, O hunter of men and slayer of fierce dragons." Josh had been gargling with eighty-six proof mouthwash and so his every word was served with a dollop of bitterness about being five feet three inches tall and having a harelip and carrot hair. It took me a long time to understand that Josh's dearest possessions were his stature, his harelip and his hair. They weren't his curses but his ticket of admission to the human circus. He felt like a sideshow performer and yearned for the big top. But he was still a performer, somehow unique, not just one of the faceless crowd. Until he could get something better in exchange for them, he'd be damned if he'd give them up. I walked past him to where I knew the prints would be. The bill said if I'd bring him the girl, he'd forget the bill. I gave him ten bucks a print, our going rate. Josh was lurching toward me. I put the prints behind my back. "She's in trouble. I know it," he slurred.

"She'll be okay, Josh. I'll find her." I wanted out and I wanted

Josh to be okay. He jabbed a freckled finger at me. "Oh yeah, the tough guy. Where's your charger, Galahad?" I knew he'd take a poke at me. I wondered whether he'd rather I take him seriously and deck him or humor him and put him in the bed he'd so obviously missed the night before. He came windmilling toward me. I ducked the blows, grabbed Josh around the waist, hoisted him over my shoulders and tossed him on the sofa.

The charade over, he looked at me. "You know how much I hate you sometimes?"

"Yeah, I know, Josh—as much as you hate yourself, so I'm in good company. Get some sleep and thanks." He waved me off and began to snore sibilantly. I picked up the folder and locked the door behind me.

I wanted a quiet place to study the prints, eat some lunch and maybe call Samantha. I cranked the car over and thought I'd go up to a nearby steakhouse. The place was dark, the tables well separated, the service unobtrusive. I hoped to beat the lunch crowd and did. A young girl in a long gown showed me to a table, took my drink order and left. When she returned with my drink I fished a print out of the folder. Josh was right. What he'd created out of my description and his own loneliness was haunting. A face of ravaged sparkle. Energy still danced in the eyes, but only there. That energy seemed to feed off her face, drawing it back into herself and then out through her eyes. She was thirteen and thirty, at the beginning and the end of her youth.

Over my steak I sorted out the pieces of the puzzle of Miranda Benson. In the past year she'd alienated her parents, stopped pursuing former interests and activities, abandoned or rejected old friends, given away things of her childhood and changed her appearance. If it had only been her parents reporting the changes, I'd have discounted part of it as ubiquitous parental dismay as their children grow up and away from them. But she seemed to be intent on shucking her previous existence, and this caterpillar was turning into a moth not a butterfly.

Becky said Randi was involved with Angie Martindale these

days and Angie Martindale sounded like a veteran mall rat. She'd be there for the starting gun. By one I figured it was time to go. I wanted to be totally familiar with the shopping center and its rhythms by the time the kids started pouring in from school. The drive over was stifling, the dry heat baking me in my car. Meat loaf under steel, the special of the day.

Chapter 8

IT WAS AFTER THREE WHEN I PULLED INTO THE SHOPPING CENTER lot and locked the car. An overturned oil tanker on the beltway had backed traffic up for miles. I felt like a pilgrim heading to a modern cathedral, one dedicated to the banishment of boredom. Three million square feet of neon lit, color-coordinated anesthetic of every shape and size. If you just keep buying things that make you happier, sexier, richer, prettier, more desirable, then the roaring, whistling emptiness that gnaws at you will go away. Right? Wrong. It's just another addiction. When you turn off the lights, the emptiness comes back. If you sit and explore your emptiness long enough you will find a handhold on your core. If you don't want to do that you get a lifetime pass to the shopping center.

I went through the doors and pulled my shirt away from my body as the first blast of air conditioning hit me. I decided to walk the length of the center's two levels and see where the kids would be likely to congregate. The first place was the Family Video Center, a cavern of pinball and electronic video games. I walked past the arcade and down the other side of the mall. The next outpost was a sporting goods store. The kids who were hanging out tended to be in the common space, not in the stores. It was either lack of money or because the real commodity on sale was a return to a giant, bright buzzing hive. Lots of other people to make contact with, to rub antennas with. I went past the shoe store to my next oases of children: the ice cream store and the puppy shop. I went down the stairs and began to stroll back down the avenue. The area outside the pizza shop was starting to attract a few kids as was a clothes boutique and the record store. I went to a drink stand, got a large 7-Up and sat down on a bench. I took out the picture and committed it to memory. I wished I had a half dozen operatives. Then I could plant one at each oasis and watch and wait. I sipped my drink and pocketed the picture. It was almost 3:30, time to hunt in earnest.

As I began my first lap I had the horrendous thought of them arriving and leaving between a circuit and my never knowing it and spending a happy day in fantasyland. I pushed the thought away and began to make my way among the crowds, comparing and discarding faces like bad draws to a poker hand. An hour and a half and four laps later, I was having a crisis of faith. I could see myself being scraped up off a bench in about six months, gibbering incoherently. All the kids were being reduced to one big, jeaned, sneakered, hairy clone and I hated them all. I closed my eyes and contemplated calling Arnie over to spell me for a while when I saw her. It was the Martindale girl. She was talking with another girl—not Cindy Fosburg—and two boys. They looked older, maybe seventeen or so. They wore sleeveless vests, homegrown tattoos and the omnipresent bulletproof wallet affixed to their belts by silver chains. One boy carried a buck knife in a clasped case on his right side. They both had spiky Mohawk haircuts and the one with the knife an attempted goatee. It was the current grits look, a hybrid produced by mating a Hell's Angel with a Punk. Its evolutionary potential was doubtful. I settled into a holding pattern on a bench on the opposite side of the corridor and hoped to intercept the girls alone. After a few minutes of giggles and nervous movements the girls moved off toward the record store. Maybe I was in luck. The store had a step-down enclosed area of benches that would afford some privacy if I could convince the girls to talk with me. I decided not to address Angie by name, as her natural suspiciousness would be heightened even more by a stranger who somehow knew her name. The girls entered the store and apparently were browsing. I stationed myself on a bench where I could see the door and hoped that all they picked up was round and vinyl. After about fifteen minutes they came out and stood in the doorway, glancing up and down, deciding which way to go. I climbed up off the bench and went toward them.

"Excuse me. May I talk with you a moment?"

The girls heads snapped around and I could see them running me through their computer systems: truant officer, cop, store detective. They were sure some past transgression was being called due. I've learned that there just isn't enough time to prove yourself trustworthy to these kids when you need information in a hurry and this may be the only time you ever pass through their lives. You can either play it straight with them and hope they'll talk to you or try to intimidate them and let the next guy attempt to pick up the pieces.

"It's about Randi Benson. I'm hoping you can help me. It'll only take a couple of minutes of your time." Now that I had become a threat once removed I could sense the tension in their bodies slacken a bit. Angie Martindale looked a lot like her picture. She still had a little baby fat on her belly and no subtlety in her clothes. Everything was tight and her sincere breasts strained her blouse with sincerity. The other girl was a washed-out brunette, whose chief distinguishing feature was two front teeth that leaned outward like a pair of tired tombstones.

"Whadaya want?" Angie whined, burdened by my request.

"I'd like to know where she is. I'd like to talk to her."

"What for? Who are you anyway?" She put her hands on her hips and turned a foot outward, a ballet of the streets.

"I'm a private detective and her parents asked me to try to find Randi." I didn't want to say they wanted me to return her if the girls had feelings on the matter.

"Right. I'll bet. Listen, with what her folks are like she's better off wherever she is."

"What are her folks like? I don't know them very well."

"They're just into keeping her a little girl, you know. Her father's all over her case, you know—about where she can go, you know, and like what she does, you know." The girl was at a loss to describe her world. She was relying on the telepathic powers of "you know" to transport her mind to mine.

"That doesn't quite sound like child abuse to me. They may not be the best parents around, or even just good enough, but why are you so sure she's better off wherever she is? There are lots of very ugly places where people can get lost." I listened to myself. Who was I kidding? This kid didn't grow up in Disneyland.

Her friend was chewing on a cuticle, worrying it like it was all she was going to get to eat.

"Look, if you know where she is and she is in such great shape, take me to her, let me see for myself. Even if I took her home, what are they going to do—chain her to the bed?" Something flicked across her eyes, not quite a flinch. I was sorry I said it. "She can always run away again." I thought to myself, if she does it often enough by the time she's sixteen nobody'll give a shit where she goes or how she gets there. "If you're not so certain she's in a great place, wouldn't you want somebody to check up on her? Wouldn't you want somebody to check up on you in a bad scene?"

She started chewing on her own nails, her eyes growing unfocused with concentration. "She left here on Friday with a guy. I don't know who he was, but he had a great car."

"Do you remember anything else about him? A name, a description, a license? How did they meet?"

"He was just hanging around and seemed to like Randi and he just came on to her, you know, talking and everything and they left together."

"What did he look like?"

"He was cute, kinda tall."

"As tall as me?"

"Yeah, but not as heavy. Kind of skinny but he had good shoulders."

Yeah. I'll bet the kind you can cry on.

"He had black hair, right, Nicky?" Her friend nodded in goggle-eyed agreement. "It was long and kind of wild. He parted it in the middle. Oh yeah, he had a gold earring in his, um, right ear. It was a little gold lion head hanging from a star in his ear."

Great, I thought. He's probably with some religious group, the Mahatma Wing Dang Doo. "What about his face? Any scars? Anything unusual—braces, glasses, a patch, you know?" God, there I go. I'm doing it. Maybe we'll just end up communicating by touching fingertips.

"No, no scars or nothing. His eyes were dark. Just real cute, you know."

"What was he wearing?" I looked around for a place to sit and motioned to a bench. They stood.

"A black muscle shirt and jeans and boots."

"Did he have any tattoos?" Like one with his name and address on it.

"Yeah, it was . . ." She giggled and snorted into her hands and doubled over. I waited it out and considered giving her a shot of estrogen to get her through this age. "It was a girl on his bicep and when he flexed, her tummy moved like she was dancing." This guy would be a snap to find if the circus was in town.

"What did he talk about? Did he mention any names?" I reminded myself to get a description of his car.

"We just talked about things, music. He was really into heavy metal." Great, the next oppressed minority. Transvestite sadomasochists unite, you have nothing to lose but your chains.

"And things, you know . . ." She broke from my gaze and stared at the floor.

"Like where to score some good dope, huh?"

"Yeah, just weed, you know. Nothing heavy."

Right he's a social worker and saving souls. "Did he talk about anything else? Any places, names?" Keep on dreaming.

"No."

"Tell me about the car. How did that come up?"

"Well, me and Nicky were leaving then too, to go to a party, and we saw this guy and Randi get into his car. It was a dark blue car, you know, with those engine things coming through the hood and all the way up in the air in the back."

"Did it have any stickers on it on the bumper?"

"Yeah, unh, one of the clubs on Route 1, Dixie's Pride, I think."

"Can you tell me anything else about it, license tag or decals?"

"No."

"Listen, you've been very helpful. Thanks very much." I reached into my wallet and came out with two of my cards. "If you think of anything else at all, I can be reached at that number at anytime. If I'm not in just leave a message." I started to walk away and then turned back. "I'll let you know if she's okay."

Unless Dixie's Pride required tattoos and earrings of everyone I was in pretty good shape. I got into my car, turned it over and pushed a tape into the player. Bruce Springsteen. The Boss. He had words for every form of exile I'd ever known.

I pulled out of the lot and headed up to the beltway. I punched the accelerator and began to climb up the ramp. I opened my window and turned up the volume. With a piano tinkling behind him, Bruce filled the evening.

I wondered what my shopping center mystery boy promised Randi Benson. Whatever it was he probably said "you know" for everything he didn't.

Chapter 9

IN TWENTY MINUTES I WAS BACK ON THE CORRIDOR. IT WAS almost six o'clock. Work was over and so the regulars at Dixie's Pride would be showing up soon. I pulled my car into the lot across the street and looked the place over. Whatever Dixie's Pride was, it wasn't fit for pubic viewing. Like a lot of other bars on Route 1, it was an ugly pillbox, squat, flat roofed, windowless—just a brick box with a door and a name over it. A pleasure bunker. I got out of my car, locked it, took a deep breath and crossed the street. I'd spent too much time in places like this to be too thrilled with a return engagement. I opened the outer door and let it close. In the darkness I reached for the inner door and entered Dixie's Pride. My brief attempt at accommodating my vision didn't really help and I groped around the tables for a second, waiting for my eyes to adjust to the inky darkness. I found a table off to the left. It was centrally located where I could watch the door and also get a sense of the layout of the place.

The walls were covered with swirling stucco. I felt like I was sitting in the middle of a giant callus. There were mirrors imbedded in all the walls. The bar took up two-thirds of the right wall. Past that was the entrance to the kitchen where Quasimodo the chef was flipping his ashes into the soup. Virginia has a bizarre rule that you have to be a restaurant to serve alcohol. The only exception to this is a half dozen bars outside the Portsmouth Naval Yard that cater to crazed seamen. The result of this rule is that some of the worst food in the universe is served in Virginia taverns. They have to maintain a ratio of receipts for food and booze, so they have to move the slop. But what goes on in the kitchens is incredible. There are sixty-five bars on the strip of Route 1 that cuts through Fairfax County and plenty of them wouldn't pass an inspection by Mr. Magoo, so somebody's getting greased somewhere. I make it a cardinal rule never to eat in a Virginia roadhouse. It is to this I attribute my old age. Past the kitchen was the fire exit and the bathrooms, I guessed. Around the tables were the first round of regulars. Mostly construction workers by their dress, but a few of the white collar boys were present. I looked around for the front man who ran this place. He was sitting at a table in the left rear corner. He had wavy blonde hair combed straight back. Empty eyes, hook nose the size of an umbrella and a cigarette that hid under it. He was going to fat and his beginning beer paunch had forced him to keep his shirt buttoned higher than was stylish down here. He had a gold necklace on that either had his name on it in case he lost himself or some drivel like peace or love. He finished off with corded slacks and patent leather shoes. He didn't look bad enough to be doubling as the muscle, so my guess was there was some monstrosity out back washing the dishes or eating them that they called on to arbitrate outbreaks of contentiousness.

The waitress found me and leaned over the table as she swept up the change and the old foam. She wore hot pants, a small halter top over large breasts and a look of terminal boredom.

"Want a menu?"

"No, just a beer."

"Schlitz is on tap."

"No. I'll take a Bud." I don't even trust the taps. Not that they'd pollute the beer, just that they'd forget to put any beer at all in the system. The stuff is so watered it doubles as the sprinkler system for fires. I figure that anything that enters in a sealed bottle is a best bet.

A red spotlight came on over the stage and the entertainment began. A girl made her way to the stage. She climbed the staircase and daintily squatted with her knees together like some lush, overripe stork or heron and put down her drink. She sprinkled some baby powder on stage and scuffed her platform shoes in it. She unclasped her gown and let it slide down her arms and she draped it across the top stair. Nude except for pasties and G-string, she stood for a moment in silence with everyone's eyes on her, waiting for the music to begin. She stared at her infinitely reflected image in the mirrored walls. I wondered if she thought she was looking at all her tomorrows. I doubt it.

When I was eighteen this was a thrill. I know the girls haven't changed so I guess the change is me. I can barely stay awake in a topless bar and I have to watch what I drink. It's not cool to fall asleep and snore at ringside. I've wandered through enough bars, massage parlors and hot-sheet motels looking for dreamers that I've had plenty of time to understand why the thrill is gone. A topless bar is no different from Disneyland, it's just selling a different illusion. The problem is that it takes a great deal of energy to sustain an illusion for a roomful of strangers twenty minutes of every hour for eight hours a day, six days a week. The illusion is that your dancing is a form of foreplay and that you are dancing for each man alone. This requires uninhibited sexuality and great physical energy. If you can dance or are attractive, so much the better. A girl who could do this would be a genius of sorts. Instead you get the zombies who can't hide that they're just doing a fifteen-dollar-an-hour job. They're about as exciting to watch as somebody electrocuting a piece of top round. They climb up on the stage and move lifelessly, their empty, glazed eyes locked on themselves in the mirror. They aren't really on stage at all.

Then there's the good old girls who may have the energy or be able to dance lively but they can't accept the idea that they're selling an illusion of personal lust for each and every guy. So they tell jokes and talk to the guys. It's just like watching your sister, nothing to it. They try to bleach all the sex out of the experience as if you were judging the Shirley Temple look-alike tap dancing contest. Every once in a great long while there's a girl who knows what she's being paid to do—or maybe she doesn't—and for a little while she has the energy, the passion. If she's attractive and can move well it's still the experience you had at eighteen. She's a magician for a short time and you are the trick. Perhaps this is why hookers call sex a trick—they're the magicians conjuring an illusion. I've never found one I could discuss this with. At least not for free.

I watched the first girl for a song or two, but I could feel an arhythmia setting in and went back to my beer. The second girl was everybody's sister. I was beginning to get terrified of the idea of eight hours in this bar watching this "show." I knew that by 2 A.M. I'd be declared brain dead. I had not seen my mystery boy come in. I hoped he'd show before my kidneys got up to leave. I was beyond nursing my beer. It was decomposing on me between sips.

The third girl walked up to the stage. She was built like some new breed of poultry: all breast and no back. She slipped off her gown and locked her arms overhead. She suddenly flexed her pectorals and her breasts jumped. She did a deep knee bend, which in five-inch heels is no mean feat, and came up, rippling her stomach and pelvis. The music began, something about "life in the fast lane" and she went to work. She swung her hips and ass from side to side, a metronome gone mad, and then did a deep squat. She bent over and pulled her tangled hair up from behind and wagged her tail at me, or so I felt. She stirred her pelvis clockwise and back again. She did a high kick and then a slow descent, as if sliding down an imaginary fire pole. She did a deep back bend, running her hands up the insides of her thighs, then across her belly. I watched her for a while as she made her way in a slow circular course during the song. She was meeting everyone's eyes boldly and turning so as to give everyone a chance to believe she only had eyes for them. When she got to me I locked eyes with her, raised my beer in tribute and let a smile escape across my face. She winked and continued to turn as she danced.

I tried to figure how to get her attention without becoming memorable. The one sure way to get a girl to talk to you is to slip her some money between dances to show how much you think of her. If the "chemistry" is right she may sit with you between sets. I figured that, being paid at fifteen dollars an hour for her time, a five spot would show I was serious but not crazy. I finished my beer and took out a five, rolled it up and put it in the mouth of the bottle. She smiled and slowly licked her lips. I was mesmerized, a mouse dancing with a rattlesnake. Bending over, she picked the bottle up and rubbed it between her breasts. She put the bill in her mouth, slowly sucking it out of the bottle while twitching her butt at the other men. She stood up, folded the bill and slowly put it in her G-string between her legs, rubbing it from side to side. I could hear it singing "Nearer My God to Thee." She winked at me again and went back to work.

I enjoyed the rest of her set and waited to see whether I'd scored or not. I had to remind myself that as much as I admired her talents she was selling illusions and I was buying hard, cold reality. In that area she could help me a lot or she could hurt me a lot.

She picked up her drink, slipped on her gown and made her way to my table.

She didn't bother to ask if she could sit. She lit her cigarette and said, "I haven't seen you in here before."

"No, and believe me, it's my loss, honey. You're something else."

"My name's Jackie. What's yours?"

"My name's Sam. Sam Thornton."

I wanted her and I didn't. She was exciting but that would wear off pretty quickly. I knew that because I had followed my impulses before. Sex is not magic. As good as it can be, as soon as it's over the world comes roaring right back at you unchanged. I know this. I'd chased long legs and big breasts for too long and had precious little to show for it. Accepting it was still not easy.

I'd push a little to get a name on my mystery boy, but not too much. If nothing came, I could always come back and wait for him to show. She was a perfect cover for my being a regular. I was smitten.

"You're the best dancer I've ever seen, let me tell you."
She smiled graciously.

"What other nights do you dance here?"

"Fridays and weekends. The other days I work at the Watering Hole."

She slowly drew a pattern on my forearm with her nails. It was getting hard to keep on track.

"Is that the one in the motel?" The place had asbestos sheets to handle the turnover. The manager only wrote half the bookings in his ledger. If the IRS knew he'd have to answer a lot of questions. If his boss found out he wouldn't get to answer any.

"Yeah. I dance and tend a little bar."

"When do you get off here?" I didn't know what I wanted her to say.

"One o'clock. But listen, man, I'm a wreck when I leave here. I just want to go home, soak my feet and hit the sack."

"How about if I catch you after a day shift?" I guess I wanted a yes. I wasn't sure I liked that.

"Okay. I'd like that. I'm on day shift Tuesday at the Hole. I get off at six." She started to slide her chair back. I reached across and put my hand on her arm and whispered, "I'm looking for a guy who hangs out here. He wears a lion's head earring, tattoo of a dancing girl. He handles some things I'm interested in. You know him?"

A razor's edge came into her eyes. She looked at me as if a fog had lifted and the prince really was a toad. She pulled away ever so slightly and avoided my eyes. Stubbing out her cigarette, she said, "No, I don't, but if I see him how can I get in touch with you?"

"My number's 555-0088. Listen, I'll see you Tuesday, huh?"

"Yeah, sure. Listen, I got to hit the head, straighten up. I'm on again in ten minutes."

"Great." She headed straight back to the bathrooms. I watched her set and then got up and left.

I went out into the cold night air. Wheels were turning. I was getting reactions. The next step would not be up to me but I would be ready. I'd wait a day for a contact and then go back to the bar to see if my wandering boy had come home.

I drove home wondering if Samantha would come over. I wanted to talk to her, to touch her. When I got in I cleared my service and got her message. I called her place. No answer. I stripped, showered and called my service. Nothing yet. I called Arnie.

"Arnie, Leo here. I think I have some work for you. Are you interested?"

"Tell me about it."

"Remember I told you about that missing kid case I've got. Well, my reading of the guy she was last with is that while he may not be Charles Manson, he's no gentleman. He sure didn't bring little Randi Benson home after they shared chocolate sodas. I'm hoping for a meeting. It'll probably be a setup and I'll want you there for backup. If the meet is amicable just tail him."

"When is all this going to go down?"

"Don't know. Can you be on standby?"

"Yeah. If that changes I'll call you."

"Fine."

I sat down at my desk and hunt and pecked out a report to Benson. I called him. No answer there either. Okay world, you don't want to hear from me. Fine! I gave Samantha another chance. She flunked. I turned in.

Chapter 10

In the morning I called my service. No messages. I read the paper while I ate a bagel with cream cheese and had a cup of coffee. That done, I called Benson.

"Hello, Mr. Benson. This is Leo Haggerty. I've got a lead on your daughter."

"Yes, what is it?"

"Friday night she left the shopping center with a boy. I have a description, no name, and a lead to a place where he hangs out. I made it clear I'm looking for him and I'm hoping to meet him soon. Maybe today. If he's still with your daughter I'll get back to you tonight with her. If not, then I'll use him to lead me to the next step. I'm getting closer. That's the best I can say."

"Jesus! Shit! What's she doing out there with this punk? You find her, Haggerty. I want her back here. Let me know as soon as you know where she is, you hear?"

"Yeah, I'll keep you posted." Benson seemed to believe that his orders would make things happen. His anxiety turned quickly to anger and demands.

I called Samantha. It rang three times and I was ready to hang up when she answered.

"Hello," she said in a sleep-thickened voice.

"Samantha, this is Leo. How are you?"

"Fine. I'm just waking up though, so I may not be too lucid."

"I got your message last night. What's up?"

"Oh, I was calling to see if I could drive by with those books I was telling you about."

"Hmmm. Good question. Things are starting to heat up on this case I've got and I may be out of touch for a while. How

57

about I call you when I know I'll be free and we can get together?"

Silence. Here we go again. Occupational Hazard number 41: finding a woman who'll settle for being a between-cases relationship. I had to admit I was getting tired of that myself. I wasn't sure I was ready for anything else, though.

"Sam, look, remember I said I kept irregular hours. Well, this is them." Nothing. I went on. "What are you thinking? Can we talk about this?"

"What I'm thinking," she said in measured tones, "is that I'm recalibrating my interest in you too. The guns scare me but I thought some more about that. I want things safe but not dull. I admit it. Maybe you can't have it both ways. Okay. But second fiddle is not a role I'm comfortable with when I'm with a man. If that's all there is I'm not sure how much I want to put into this. That's what I'm thinking right now."

I could feel this relationship slipping away from me like so many others. Always the same sticking points. Before I'd always been secretly relieved that they were ending. I'd just go on moving through an endless field of women. They were still out there. I was finally getting tired of always moving on. Maybe I was ready to find out what it took to settle down. To wake up knowing where you stood every day.

"I'm not sure what it is I've got to offer a woman. I'm not even sure anymore what I need from them. I do know I'd love to find out with you. It may still be second fiddle to my work. But for the first time in my life I'm not sure that's the way I want it. What do you say we just keep at this and not write it off over the phone?"

"I wasn't writing this off, just rethinking how much to put into it, that's all."

"I'll call you when I can. You call me when you want. If we can get together I'd like that. A lot. Hold on to the books. I will get them from you. Okay?"

"Yeah, it's okay." She stopped for a second. "Leo, be careful, damn you." Then she hung up the phone.

I set down the receiver feeling like 400 pounds were sitting on my throat.

I spent the rest of the day looking for Randi Benson in all the conventional ways. I talked to Cindy Fosburg's older sister who told me that Cindy was in the juvenile detention center in Fairfax and had been for almost a week. No help there. I wandered in and out of every topless bar on the corridor looking for a guy with a tattooed bicep and a lion's head earring. No such luck. I talked to every speed shop mechanic I could find about a jacked up blue car with an air scoop. Nothing.

At six I packed it in and went home. I'd just walked in and was holding a cold bottle of beer to my forehead when the call came in.

"Haggerty," a flat voice said. "I know you been asking for me. Meet me at the Princess Cinema. You know the fuck film joint. Be there for the 7:30 show. Come while the lights are on. Sit in the seat next to the aisle one, next-to-the-last row, left side and keep both hands on the back of the seat in front of you."

I called Arnie. "We got a bite, the Princess Cinema. Be there lights on, a specific seat, hands in view. What happened to honor among thieves? He wants me next-to-last row, a seat from the aisle. Why don't you sit at the other end of the row in front of me. Come ten minutes early to the 7:30 show. I'll sit with my feet under the seat in front of me. Okay? Any questions?"

"Yeah, just one."

"What?"

"What's playing?"

"I don't know. Look it up in coming attractions."

"That's terrible, Leo. See you there."

I began to get ready for my date. I flipped my wallet out on the desk. I didn't want any ID on me when this went down. I dressed all in black and checked my gun. I was carrying the Colt .45 now that Arnie had modified it. I slipped it cocked and locked into my shoulder holster. I went to my dresser and got my backup piece, a Beretta and its holster. Sitting on the bed I strapped the holster onto my left ankle. I stood up and adjusted it and pulled my black slacks down over it. I checked myself in the mirror: the well-dressed pigeon goes out on the town.

Chapter 11

I WENT DOWN TO MY CAR AND HEADED OVER TO THE THEATER. A porno theater is a good place for a meet. It's full of lonely guys wishing their wives or somebody would do what that girl on the screen was doing and they're guilty as hell about that. So they sit with their heads locked, eyes front, sure that their mother is searching the aisles for them. They're all playing with themselves or trying not to. To look at another guy, especially one at work, is tacky to say the least. So a guy making funny noises, like you do when you're swallowing your teeth, is the last person anybody is going to look at.

I pulled into the lot and looked at the theater. The feature was called *Tail Pipe*. I hoped Arnie wasn't going to be bored. The theater was located between a Vietnamese restaurant and an ABC store.

I locked my car and walked across the lot to the theater. A skinny blonde with streaked hair and bad teeth told me through a cigarette haze that *Tail Pipe* would begin in about five minutes and it was three dollars. I paid my way and went in. There was a sprinkling of guys, eyes front, listening to the inane Muzak. I saw the seat I was to take. As I walked to it I saw Arnie slumped over, looking almost asleep at the other end of the aisle in front of me. I sat down and slid my feet under the seat in front of me. I extended my arms and put my hands on the back of the seat in front of me. I figured he'd wait in the dark for a few minutes to get his night vision. The lights went out and the screen lit up.

The movie began. Behind the credits on the screen, a blonde woman grasped a penis with her hand. Her scarlet nails were two inches long. They encircled the shaft like a parrot's claw. She eyed the cock hungrily and dove on it, her head bobbing with the ferocity of a starving bird wrestling with the last worm on earth. The camera panned back and this scene became a movie scene being viewed by an assorted group of men and women.

I waited eyes front. Nobody sat next to me. My arms were getting stiff. A good move on his part. If this was a joke, I was going to be very pissed. I presumed he was somewhere nearby watching me. How long he was going to wait was up to him. I decided to sit through the flick and leave if no one showed.

As in most of these movies, the plot seemed to move toward the creation of some giant flesh engine composed mostly of pumping piston rods and varied intake valves. Its operation seemed to produce little else than a shuddering in place and a groaning exhaust. Simple but effective.

A man sat down next to me. I turned to look at him. He drove a right into my solar plexus. I gasped forward, my jaw pulled down. A fire of pain radiated through my chest, crawling up my throat. I was too paralyzed to speak. A solar plexus shot not only delivers the pain, it keeps it quiet too; sealed behind the paralyzed vocal cords. My brain felt like it was on a runaway merry-go-round. I wished I could pick a sound out of the blur and mail it to my tongue. Hands patted me down, lifting out my .45. Far away down a cotton tunnel someone said I was clean. The guy who hit me was sitting on the aisle seat with my piece pointed right at me. I heard someone sliding into the seat behind me. A hand grabbed my hair and rammed my head against the edge of the seat in front of me. Stars erupted behind my eyes and it was the Fourth of July in my head.

"All-right, asshole, I got a message for you." The man behind me hissed in my ear. "Stop looking for trouble. Drop what you're doin'. Got it?"

I got my head rapped against the metal seat for that. When my head bounced back I looked for Arnie. He was gone. No one else in the theater was paying us any attention. I felt like Kitty Genovese.

"Do you understand, shit-for-brains?" My head bounced off the seat back again. I couldn't take much more of this. My ears were ringing. I said I understood. There was a tap on my instep. I slid my feet back under me.

"Good. It's been a pleasure talking to you. I think it's time we all left." He giggled breathlessly.

The man next to me raised my Colt and put it under my jawbone as if to lift me out of my seat by it. I rasped out of the side of my mouth, "The guy behind you with the twelve gauge pointed at your head says no." The man behind me never even flinched. Instead he laughed. "That's good, shit-for-brains. I'd do the same in your shoes but there's no one there, hee hee."

"Kiss your brains good-bye," I said. The guy sitting next to me snuck a glance over his shoulder into the dark. I rolled off the edge of his gun as a silver blur arced over my head. The edge of a gun barrel had cut through the cheeks, flattened the nose and taken out several teeth of the man next to me, spurting blood all over both of us. I had rolled off the seat as Arnie had come up off the floor of the row in front of us. He swung back and leveled his giant .45 Magnum at the man behind me. The guy with the broken face moaned softly in his seat, his head lolling back. I picked up my piece and went to the guy in the seat behind me and stuck it in his ear. "Walk or die here, asshole, your choice." It was hard not to see three of him. Wouldn't somebody get that phone?

He levered himself out of the chair. I stuck my gun in his ribs and followed him out. Arnie was undoing the other guy's collar, pulling his jaw up and tilting his head back. "Come on. What're you doing?" Arnie was still looking at the man.

"Making sure he doesn't choke on his blood. I'd hate to kill someone I didn't mean to."

In the parking lot I frisked the guy. No ID and one .357 Magnum. I fished in the guy's pockets for his car keys. "Which one is it?" He stonewalled. "You want to die here?"

"Blue one, over there." I pushed him toward his car and

handed his gun to Arnie. After I unlocked the door Arnie shoved the guy in the back seat of the car and got in next to him. We left the lot and headed west.

I looked at our guest. He was big. He had me by an inch or two and maybe twenty pounds. He was a forelock away from being totally bald and that rose from his head like a dorsal fin. A toothpick danced in the corner of his mouth like a conductor's baton.

"Okay, shit-for-brains, my turn to play. Who sicked you on me?"

"Fuck off."

"Who's the guy with the lion head earring?"

Nothing, just a glare.

"Is it the chicks? He's a chicken hawk maybe?"

Still nothing.

"Okay, tough guy. I ain't gonna waste my time with you. You had your chance to talk. Now it's your chance to die."

Arnie grinned at my friend. He just stared hatefully back.

In Annandale we found an open car wash. I paid for a wash and got on the tracks. We entered the machine and were immersed in a spray of hot soapy water. A rod with long soft sponges attached to it moved over the car like a chorus line of dancing octopi. It was silent in the car, the motor was off, the windows up, just coasting on the rollers. I looked back at my friend, then at Arnie, then back at my friend. He stared impassively at us, his lips set. "Do it."

Arnie waited a second and then pulled the hammer back.

"Okay. Okay. I'll talk. Sweet Jesus, don't kill me."

"All right. Who sent you?"

"I don't know. I got a phone call. Some guy said you were causing trouble looking for some guy. He didn't use no names. He told me to scare you off. He didn't care how."

"How much were you paid?"

"Five hundred up front. Another five if you got the message."

"How'd you get the money?"

"It was in my mailbox the next day. Cash. Five C notes."

"Who was the other schmuck with you?"

"My brother."

"You do this kind of work often?"

"Jesus man. It weren't personal. Just a job. I mean, Christ, I been laid off two months. Construction's really hurtin'."

The Reagonomics of evil. When the cost of living goes up, the price of dying comes down. If my head didn't hurt so much holding it still, I think I'd have jumped over the seat and beaten the shit out of him. "Okay, sport. You've been such a big help, let's go for the sixty-four-thousand-dollar question. What's your name?"

He looked at me weakly. "Chuck Campbell."

"And your brother's?"

"Steve. Steve Campbell."

"Very good. Now how do we know this whole fairy tale is true?"

"Man, I wouldn't shit you. You could kill me."

"That's right. So if this guy contacts you again I'll know about it, right, Chuckie baby?"

"Yeah. Sure. Whatever you say."

We left the car wash and drove in silence for a while. Then I stopped at a phone booth on Braddock Road. I looked up Campbell, Charles in the phone book and called the number. His wife said yes, Chuck and his brother would both be interested in a job. And yes, it had been tough being laid off so long, and yes, heavy equipment operators were the first to go. I thanked her for her time, hung up and got back in the car.

"Nice woman, your wife, Mr. Campbell. Let's keep her that way, shall we?"

Chuck's head bobbed rapidly. I turned back to the road and started the engine. Twenty minutes later we were back at the movie house. I took the keys out and turned to Campbell. "One last thing. The five hundred, fork it over."

He stared at me in disbelief. "Chuck, please let's not make it hard on yourself. It's just bad policy to let other people profit at my expense."

He looked at Arnie and saw no help there. Reaching into his jacket he came out with a money clip. I took the five hundred out and gave the clip to him. As I got out of the car I stuck my head back in and tossed Chuck his keys. As he reached down for them I punched him right in the nose. He fell back moaning on the seat.

"Oh yeah, Chuck. Remember, it's nothing personal, just a job."

Blood was running between his fingers. Good. I rubbed my forehead. It was feeling better already.

Chapter **12**

I GOT INTO ARNIE'S CAR. HE TURNED THE MOTOR OVER AND SAID, "What now?"

"We pay a visit to a girl with loose lips, amigo."

Arnie gunned it down Duke Street over the Telegraph Road overpass then down Kings Highway to Route 1. We pulled into a gas station and I called the Watering Hole. After two rings a whiny voice said "The Hole. Yeah?"

"Listen, is Jackie there?"

"Nah, she just went off."

"Do you know where she went?"

"Nah. Waddaya want?"

"Listen, I got her outfit fixed up, the leather one. She wanted to try it out, I just want to drop it by for her."

"All right. Lemme ask a minute."

I stood in the phone booth, looking at the shredded book. I was getting parboiled in the heat, cooked in my own juices.

The whine returned. "She was in the lounge talking to some guy. She'll be back in about fifteen, twenty minutes. You could leave it at the desk."

"Okay. Thanks."

I pushed back the glass door and wiped my brow. I wished to hell I favored an ankle piece, this coat was killing me. I slid back in the car with Arnie.

He looked at me expectantly. "Well?"

"She's not on stage. She was in the bar. She ain't now but she'll be back."

"What do you think?" Arnie went for the ignition.

"I think she's a semi-pro and she's turning a quick one out of

66

the bar before she splits. Maybe it's the first of the night. I think she's upstairs. Let's go pay her a call. If she's working upstairs, we'll go up the fire escape and look for her. There are only two floors upstairs. All the rooms are off the corridor." I knew the place all too well.

Arnie nodded and we drove past the motel up an adjoining street to its rear. The Watering Hole was a three story box with a topless bar on the first floor and the rapid turnover rooms upstairs. The place was a firetrap; no sprinkler system, no fire doors. The paint was peeling. There were piles of garbage in the halls. The rooms were very elegant: no TVs, no phones, no linens, no lamps, no chairs. Just a bed with stained sheets, a dilapidated dresser, a moldy shower and toilet, cracked linoleum and constant drips. They were honest rooms though. There were no Bibles. The cops know that it's a "trick motel" but they don't touch it. In the past fourteen years plenty of high school kids had celebrated graduation in its rooms.

We pulled up in back, parked and walked back down the street. Then we went through a hole in the fence to the back of the lot next to the Dempsey dumpster. The fire escape was pulled up. I jumped up and grabbed the end. It swung down. Arnie climbed up after me. We went to the second floor and tried the door. It was locked on the outside. Great. A nice place to fry. We went up to the third floor. The door there opened. Standing in the hall we each took one side and moved from door to door, listening for love. Arnie stopped at the second door. Then he moved away. I crossed the hall to him and he said, "Snoring."

We went down to the second floor and began to work our way back toward the rear. Midway back on the left side, I stopped. Inside the bed sang and people were gasping in harmony.

I pulled out my gun and Arnie did the same. I knew from previous sorties that the bed would most likely be against the far wall. I reached down and tried the handle. Locked. I picked it with a credit card. Arnie and I glanced at each other and nodded. The groaning increased as did the bed's bouncing cacophony. I turned the handle and opened the door slightly. Jackie was heels to heaven, hard at work. On top of her was a chubby guy with thin, longish hair and an adolescent's corrugated complexion. He was beginning to jerk spasmodically, so his ride was about to end. Jackie was lying back, moaning "ooh, baby," her eyes closed, probably doing a cost-benefit analysis on the latest fifteen minutes of her life. I was disappointed. She was about as discriminating as a light socket. If you could get it up, you could get it in. I pulled up alongside her consort and stuck my gun in his ear. He pulled his head back like it had been burned and stared at the .45's snout. He whimpered, "Oh Jesus." Jackie's eyes lit up but before she could scream Arnie stuck his gun in her face. She moved her eyes up his arm and didn't like what she saw.

I told him, "This is a no-parking zone. Now I want you to back out and go stand in the shower with the water on high and your head under it. What you don't know might save your life."

He backed out and off the bed. He was maybe nineteen years old, a soft, pimply, dirty kid who was gonna mess himself if he didn't hurry. He hopped to the bathroom holding his peter. As I turned back to Jackie Arnie went to the bathroom to keep an eye on her friend. Jackie had lowered her legs and pulled the covers up over her tits. I sat on the edge of the bed and looked at her, never moving the gun from a line right between her eyes. "You know, Jackie, we have a problem. You see, you tried to feed me to the sharks. Now that's what any little fishy would do. I don't blame you but the problem is I ate the sharks and now I'm gonna take a bite out of you. I want to know where the guy with the lion head earring is?"

"I don't know," she said, her voice going soft and childlike. An appeal to my decency. My head throbbed.

"Look, cunt, we can do this the easy way or the hard way. My friend here would love to be every bad dream you've ever had. I let him have you and you'll end up looking like a tray of cold cuts and I'll still get what I want. The easy way is you tell me now and then you get dressed and packed and leave town right away because they'll know who talked." I watched her calculate her chances. She wasn't brave and she didn't have any power. It was just a question of who was going to swat her.

She stared at me, trying to read my face. Would I kill her anyway? Would I really kill her? Which way was out? I met her eyes and tried to see her as a bug. It worked.

"All right, all right, damn it. The guy works for Monte Panczak." She spit the words out as if trying to put some distance between herself and them.

"Not good enough. That's like saying he works for the government. Where does he work? What does he do for Monte?" I let my face soften, as much for myself as her.

"You know Rowdy's down on Route 1?" I nodded. "Well, he works there. He does a little of everything. Tends the bar. Keeps the books. You know—arranges things."

"What else do you know about him? His name, where he lives, friends, everything."

"Uh, his name's Tony, Tony Julian. Uh, he lives off Route 1 somewhere, Hybla Valley maybe. Listen, I never got it on with him or nothing. I don't know where he lives."

"What's his work schedule?"

"I don't know. He just seems to drop in and out when he feels like it. Takes a lot of calls at the bar."

"Who do you see him with? Any friends in particular? A girlfriend?"

"No, he's friends with everybody. No, no girlfriend. He scores with lots of chicks. Anything he wants, he's real cool." The scorn in her voice burned through her words.

"What would he want with a thirteen-year-old girl then?" I said it as if it were a fact asking for embellishment, not a question to be rejected.

"How would I know?" she bleated.

"Because I asked you about him and then two muscle heads tried to dance on my face. You told someone I was interested in this schmuck and somebody doesn't want anyone interested in him. I know he's got a thirteen-year-old girl with him. Now one last time the easy way, what for?"

"I don't know what you're talking about, honest. And I didn't tell anyone anything about you. That's the god's-honest truth."

She flicked a look at Arnie who shook his head sadly. "Okay, okay. Jesus you gotta help me if I tell you this. I mean, they'll kill me."

"All right. I said I would. Just tell me about this guy."

"Okay. Tony works for Monte Panczak. I told you that. Well, Monte runs a lot of things: the topless bars around Fort Belvoir and a lot of outcall massage parlors. That stuff just fronts for a lot of hooking. He's got a whole string of girls working for him. Well, Tony kind of, you know, recruits for him. He looks for girls hanging out on Route 1—chicks who need the money—and he gets them started."

"Are they running a ring of little kids?"

"I don't know. Maybe he didn't know she was thirteen. Christ, some of these kids grow up so fast you can't tell." She sounded genuinely rueful. Perhaps the competition was getting to her.

"No, he'd find out. Kiddie fucking is about the only thing people still frown on. They'd find out. It's too big a risk to take stupidly." Where would they work a girl like this? Off a phone joint, of course. Keep her off the streets. "How many outcall places does Panczak run?"

"I don't know. Six or seven in Alexandria and here."

She was starting to run down. The adrenaline surge that came with talking to me was starting to wear off. I had to decide whether threats or kindness would be more effective in keeping her tongue wagging. I reached over to the pack of cigarettes on the nightstand, shook one out, gave it to her and lit it for her. She took a shuddering breath and slowly blew out the smoke. Her hand was trembling and she bunched the covers in front of her.

"Arnie, go out to the phone booth in the hall and get the phone book."

He nodded and left.

70

Jackie looked at me. "Would he really cut me? I mean, Jesus, I've tried to help. You said you wouldn't hurt me, right? I mean, I'll do anything you want." She let the covers drop and held her breasts up to me. "I'll do both of you. Any way you like. Just please don't hurt me." She started to cry and buried her face in her hands.

I ran my hand through my hair. What the hell am I doing here? I thought. I handed her back the covers.

"You're doing fine and if you keep that up you'll walk out of here in one piece. We'll never tell who gave us the information. But I'd suggest you relocate real soon. Oh, by the way, yes, he would do it and no, he wouldn't think twice about it." That was a lie but one I still wanted her to believe. Just as I'd wanted Chuck Campbell to believe that Arnie would have shot him in the car wash.

Arnie returned and threw the book on the bed, complete with its snapped security chain. I flipped it open to massage parlors and said, "Okay, which ones are Panczak's?" I gave her a pen to check them. While she did that I opened her purse and fished around for her wallet. She had no ID with her. She finished and looked up at me. "Does he use any of these as a specialty shop?"

"I don't know, honest I don't. I work the topless clubs and free-lance a little. I never worked outcall. Shit, I don't like sex that much. I only do this when I really need the dough."

"All right, all right." I fished the folded C notes out of my wallet and held them out to her. "Thanks for your help. Now be smart and be gone. These'll help you start over."

She took the money, slid out of bed and grabbed her dress, pulling it on quickly over her head without adjusting it to her plateaus and ridges. She slipped into her shoes, picked up her bag and skittered out the door.

I reached over to the bed, grabbed the phone book and ripped out the massage parlor pages. As I turned to leave, Arnie motioned to the shower. I handed him the pages from the phone book.

"Right, yes." I stepped into the bathroom and turned off the water. The upright prune looked up at me saucer-eyed. I stuck out my hand and Arnie filled it with the kid's wallet. I flipped it open to his driver's license. "Okay, Jeff Melton, I know who you are and where you live. Life will stay pleasantly dull for you so long as you remember you were never here and heard nothing? Got it?"

His head bobbed agreement and I flipped him his wallet. Arnie and I left the way we came.

Chapter 13

"OKAY, WHERE TO NOW?" ARNIE SAID AS WE SLID OUT OF THE woods behind the motel.

"A phone booth. I want to call the cops."

Arnie looked at me quizzically.

"Actually a cop—Frank Schaefer—and ask him some questions about Monte Panczak and the mob."

We stopped on Route 1 at an Exxon station and I got into the phone booth and called the police.

"Fairfax County Police. May I help you?"

"Yes. Is Lieutenant Schaefer there?"

"May I say who's calling?"

"Leo Haggerty."

As she tried to reach Frank Schaefer, I stood in the phone booth reading the obscenities on the walls. Wanda liked gang bangs and could be reached at , . .

"Hello, Leo. What's happening?"

"Nothing much, Frank. I just want to know if Monte Panczak is connected to the mob?"

"And why would you want to know that, Leo?"

"It's a case I'm on."

"Tell me about it."

"No, no can do that."

"Pretty please."

"C'mon, Frank. I've got nothing of use to you. If I can turn anything over to you, you know I will. Just tell me about Panczak. He's on the edge of this case and I'd just like to know who I'm irritating if I have to."

"Okay. Look, it's a long tale. I'm leaving for a bite to eat. How about we catch the chicks at Dixie's Pride and talk there?"

"Uh, no, Frank. I'm persona non grata there right now. How about some wholesome family food at the Pig?"

"Okay."

"Fine, we'll be in a corner booth."

Frank came in, looked around morosely at the spick-and-span dining room but grinned when one of the waitresses called him "honey." We waved him over.

Frank was in his late thirties. He was well dressed in his three-piece suit. Apart from the three "V"-shaped scars under his eyes he looked like a typical upwardly mobile professional: real estate, accounting, what have you. The scars came from a kid who'd had enough PCP in him to turn his brain into fertilizer.

He stopped at the table and spread his arms out, palms up. "Well, look at him—the famous shamus, the Sam Spade of Fairfax County. Christ, Leo, for a while I thought I'd never get away from your face, TV interviews, newspaper stories. Is it true they're going to make a movie about it with Nick Nolte as you? Would you sign my napkin, please?"

"Gimme a break, Frank, and sit down."

As he started to sit he said, "Bullshit and envy aside, that was a nice piece of work you did on the Saunders case."

"Thanks, Frank."

He took off his glasses and rubbed his eyes.

"You don't look so hot, Frank. Something the matter?"

Frank looked off out the window into the parking lot. "You know I'm not sure what kind of animals are out there anymore. It's getting more insane every day. Now we've got designer criminals, regular fuckin' Pierre Cardins." He stopped for a second and took a sip of water.

"Right after you called it came in. The seventh one, damn it. We got this nut we call the refrigerator rapist. He rapes women in their homes. Then for garnish he leaves something in them from the refrigerator. Last week an eight-year-old girl came home from school to find her mother tied to the kitchen table with a zucchini sticking out of her. Bastard was real cute, a fucking comedian. Cut the word 'vegina' on her belly. What kind of creature does something like that?"

There was no adequate answer. None of us tried for one.

Frank took a deep breath and shook his head sadly. "Well, Leo, what can I do for you regarding Mr. Panczak?"

"Tell me about him, his operations. Is he free lance or connected with the mob? I know he's got some outcall places and topless bars. Is he into anything else?"

"No, he's got a one-track mind. Sex is his bag. He's like a shark with those fish around its mouth. What do you call them."

"Remoras."

"Yeah. He cruises around with these scumbags sucking the garbage off his lips. They do a little blackmail here and there, some extortion of smaller operators. He's got some topflight muscle working for him."

"Where does he stand in the vice hierarchy?"

"He's a middle man trying to move up to the big time. He's running all the action in northern Virginia right now: the combat zone around Belvoir and the massage parlors in Alexandria. He gets protection money from any small-time independents over here or he busts their heads. I think he pays for his piece of the act up the line. Who to, I don't know. Believe me, he minds his manners. If any of the boys in New York thought he was getting greedy, he'd be taking all of his meals through a tube. He's probably in their good graces. They like centralization, order, peace and profits and he's brought all that to them. So as long as he's willing to be the Duke of Fairfax and doesn't threaten the big boys he'll do well. If someone tried to muscle in on him he'd have no problem getting some out-of-town talent to keep the peace. He keeps his nose clean, takes his piece, pays the big boys and lives real well."

"Where does he live?"

"Where else but that bastion of breeding, Potomac Bluffs. Big old house on about five acres of land overlooking the river. Can you imagine him at the country club. "Excuse me, Mrs.

Lethbridge. This is your neighbor, Mr. Panczak, the noted pimp? Oh, he keeps a low profile, does everything right. He's got so many corporations all tied up to each other it looks like a daisy chain for octopuses. He has the best legal talent money can buy. If I even put my hands on Monte's lapels I get one of those blow-dry shitheads screaming 'police brutality' in my ear. I wonder how they feel about their client having an electric curling iron stuck up the cunt of a recalcitrant employee?" Frank was trying to turn the table into sawdust and his intensity had created a zone of stillness around us as if all the air had been sucked in to feed his flames. Fortunately, we weren't overheard and the waitress gingerly stepped up to take our orders.

When she left, Frank exhaled and put his hands palms down on the table. He said, "See, I'm in control, this stuff doesn't get to me. My stress management courses are working wonders, right? Shit. I'd love to bust one of those bastards. I'd sleep like a baby. I might even have good dreams."

"Hell, Frank, you do your best to contain the shit. That's all you can do. I know how you feel. I can pick and choose the trash pits I work in. It adds to your life span."

"Yeah, yeah. I know, I know."

"Listen, Frank, can you tell me what you've got going on Panczak?"

"I can't, Leo. Look, as far as the front end of his operation goes, nobody gives a shit what he does. They can do it in the street. It's the back room that people are interested in. Not busting hookers or burning up tons of trash, but using the porn connection to take a bite out of organized crime. The RICO statutes give us a handle to pry into the mob's money. We think they filter a lot of money through it. Did you know it grosses four billion dollars a year? So we try to work back to the money men at the top. Hell, they could just as well be running St. Guido's home for the mentally retarded. We don't care about the front. It's because you can empty the coffers of the mob and knock down some of the big boys—that's why anything at all is done about porn." Frank stopped talking as the waitress brought our beers, a pile of barbecued ribs and fries.

"Anyway, think about it. You can add up what's probably going on. But, yeah, we're looking at Monte Panczak among others."

"Okay, Frank, I know nobody gives a shit about pornography. Only a couple of things that still turn people off: kiddie porn and kiddie hookers. Any of that around?"

"Well, well, Leo. What're you sniffing around at, old boy?" He leaned forward with a gleam in his eye and took a huge bite out of a rib.

"Nothing, Frank. I've just heard some tangential stuff about Panczak in my work on a case and I wondered if you could verify it."

"Right, Leo, of course—idle curiosity. I'll let it pass now, but believe me if you tumble on to something I want to know about and fast. Capische?"

"Understood. So what's the word."

"Nothing. Just straight hooking. They run a specialty shop up on Washington Street. You can get a chick to piss on your head if that's what you want, but kiddies, no. Panczak's smart. He takes only big benefit risks. His outcall places earned him a million bucks last year. Whatever earns lots of money, is low on a prosecutor's priorities, and he can hide from in a corporate mess he'll do. But kiddies—that still rankles a few in the Sovereign Commonwealth of Virginia, and I think he'd steer clear of that. But I'd love him to fuck up like that and float his ass downriver forever. Oh, that is a nice thought." Frank finished a rib and looked up at Arnie, who had sat silently through the whole meeting. Their eyes met and as Frank was breaking his away Arnie spoke.

"What happened to your face?"

Frank looked at Arnie's topknot and mustache and said slowly, "A kid thought my eyes were shooting fire at him so he tried to take them out with a bottle opener." Frank patted his mouth and added, "must've made sense to the kid cause he sure as hell had ice in his eyes."

Arnie said, "What happened?"

"He was on top of me trying to open my face. I shot him three times in the chest real close. This big gush of blood came out of his mouth all over me. I can still see it sometimes." His eyes refocused on us. "It's better than it used to be. Used to be I could feel it all over me. Leo, you take care now and keep in touch." Frank excused himself and left.

"Well, Leo, what now?"

"We think about what we've learned. First of all, we know Panczak isn't the mob. He coexists but is not connected. Two, nobody including the people who are looking at him know of any kiddie action. Three, he lives in Potomac Bluffs. Four, he's cautious and doesn't like risks. Five, the specialty shop is on Washington Street."

I went on. "Let's put it together with the rest of what we know so far. Tony Julian works for Panczak. He recruits chippies. A kind of 'Uncle Monte wants you!' Panczak doesn't take chances that we know of. Maybe Julian found out how old she was and he's using her himself—a little free-lance action. If so, Panczak would be very pissed at that. He might even clear the way for us to take Julian off if he thought he'd been compromised that way. That's our first order of business: sort out whose scene this is, Panczak's or Julian's. If Monte's not doing it he'll be very upset if he takes a tumble for it. I'd rather not be the 'ravell'd sleave of care' for someone like Panczak. He just might decide to stitch it up with .45 caliber yarn."

Arnie kept eating while I talked. Then he said, "I think there's another piece that we know. Chuck Campbell. From what Schaefer said, Panczak can call in first line pros from New York if he wants. Why use an amateur like Campbell? That sounds like Tony Julian scratching around for some local talent to me."

"Good point. I just want to be as sure as I can about what we're getting into. Once we find out who's running this gig we've got to see if it's live or film. If Panczak is in this it's probably films. The profit margin is so much higher. One fuck film and you can make countless copies. It'll play forever. On celluloid the kids never get older. Julian would probably be running live action. It's more portable; less overhead, lower security risks."

"Leo, don't forget there may be nothing here at all. This guy Julian could be fucking the beauteous Randi and be keeping her on ice because she's thirteen and the courts frown on true love between adults and wee children. It may be no more than that."

"Right and I'm Mr. Rogers. This kid was last seen with the chief procurer of the area's biggest whoremaster. Since then they've both vanished. They're working her one way or another."

"I don't care what Frank says. If their intelligence was so good they'd have closed Monte down by now. I think we have to cover all the bases. For live action we ought to just order Randi up and see if Panczak can deliver. If so, we just walk off with the kid. If he doesn't have her we'll try Julian the same way. A film setup stinks; we'll try that route last. Let me have that list of massage palors Jackie gave us—see if any one is on Washington Street."

Arnie pulled out the yellow pages, unfolded them and passed them to me. I scanned each page. "Here we are, Garden of Eden Health Salon."

We paid the check, left our tip and strolled out of the Pig, looking to set up a date with a thirteen-year-old hooker. Arnie drove me back to my car at the theater. I told him I'd call tomorrow morning with the details of the meet. We split up and I drove back to my house. I typed up a report and a bill for Benson and called him.

"Hello. Mr. Benson? Leo Haggerty here. I know it's quite late but I thought you'd want to know that I've made some progress in locating your daughter. I now have the name of the boy she was last with. I'm hoping to catch up with him tomorrow." I thought I'd spare Benson my grimmest fears.

"Fine. Fine. Sounds like it's been pretty easy going so far."

"Yeah. Nothing unusual about this case yet." If you were Spiderman, maybe.

"Uh, you keep me posted on things, okay?"

"Sure. I've prepared a report and an expense sheet to date. I'll mail it out to you tomorrow. It's been three full days today."

"How long do you think this'll take to wrap up?"

"Three more days is my guess."

"Okay. I'll send you another check tomorrow."

"Fine. I'll be in touch."

I pushed back from the desk, went into the kitchen and poured myself a glass of Power's Irish Whiskey. I leaned back in my stressless chair, darkened the room and closed my eyes. Today just wouldn't go away. Once upon a time this was romantic to me. Sitting alone holding a grudge against the world for disappointing me. Savoring it like a fine brandy that only improves with age. Somewhere between my head, Steve Campbell's teeth, Frank Schaefer's tale and Jackie's begging me not to hurt her, today got out of hand. I wanted to come home to something more than a dark and empty house, to sit in with a pain behind my eyes. I went to the phone.

"Hello, Sam? This is Leo."

"Hi. I'm surprised to hear from you. Is everything cleared up?"

"No, not hardly. At least this case isn't clearing up. I know it's real late but I'd like to see you."

"Are you sure?"

"Yeah. I'm sure."

"Okay. I'll be there in about a half-hour."

I paced around as if I were waiting for the first precinct reports on judgment day. My head was still pounding if I moved too fast. I went to the bathroom for some aspirin. My forehead was sore and purple. I wanted to hit Chuckie boy again.

Samantha was right on time. I let her in and stood there admiring her. A sporty little model in basic black and white. White designer jeans, black T-shirt and sandals. We kissed. It felt more natural this time. Stepping back, she reached overhead and stretched herself. I could hear her spine crackle.

"Oh, that feels good. All day over a typewriter and I feel like the Hunchback of Notre Dame."

"How did the writing go?"

"It was a good day. One of those times when the hand guides itself. It just seems to have a life of its own. It's almost like being in a trance. When that happens I try to stay with it until the spell is broken. Then I quit. How about you?"

"Interesting."

"I can see interesting. It's written all over your face. In black and blue letters. What happened to your head?"

"I tried to refinish a chair with it."

"Very funny."

"No. Somebody tried to scare me off this case, but it didn't work. I'm getting closer. I can feel it. I also have a bad feeling that this kid is in deep shit."

"How so?"

"Hooking. She's thirteen, for Christ sakes."

Samantha hugged herself and turned away. "That's terrible."

She looked at me closely. "You look terrible and I don't mean your head. What happened today? I think I'd like something to drink."

"I'll get it for you. What do you want?"

"Some wine—white if you've got it."

"Coming up." I went into the kitchen, poured her a glass of the house white, came back and handed it to her.

I sat down on the sofa and patted the seat so she would join me. She declined and sat facing me in another chair.

"Today got real confusing. The victims and the villains started changing places on me. About the only difference between them is who's feeling the pain, and that's about as clear cut as sunrise. First, you're looking at one thing, then it's something else and when it changed you can't even say. Someday I'm going to make a big mistake and that worries me." I stopped and sipped my drink. "Anyway, I just felt like having somebody to say that to."

Samantha smiled at me and her eyes crinkled. "I'm glad you did." I felt like I'd been bathed in warm butterscotch. God bless wise eyes and a warm smile. I thought that maybe I'd stop looking for long legs and big breasts. Maybe I was growing up.

Samantha looked down at the floor for a second and did fingernail laps around her glass. She looked up. "Oh, by the way, I have something for you." She reached into her purse and pulled out three books. I leaned forward and took them from her.

"Thank you." I looked at them: *Machine Dreams* by Jayne Anne Phillips; *Bodily Harm* by Margaret Atwood and *Dinner at the Homesick Restaurant* by Anne Tyler.

I stared out into space for a while. Samantha sipped her wine and watched me. Rain began to tap on the roof. I went over to the curtains, drew them back and opened the sliding glass patio doors.

"I love the sound of rain late at night. I find it incredibly soothing."

"I know what you mean; it affects me the same way."

We sat and listened to the rain beat on the roof and against the glass doors.

"What are you going to do next?" she asked.

"Oh, I'll try to arrange a date with this girl through one of the outcall services. If that doesn't get me anywhere I'll keep looking for the guy who recruited her, maybe bait him with another girl that looks like the one I'm looking for. Just keep turning over rocks and see what crawls out. This job is mostly persistence and patience.

"Why don't you scoot your chair up here, Sam. You'll hear the rain better."

She pursed her lips and then slid her chair alongside mine.

"Leo."

"Yeah."

"Please don't call me Sam again." Her tone indicated that I'd tripped over an emotional land mine.

"Okay. Sure. I'll just call you Samantha, no problem."

"Thanks. Maybe I'll feel different about this later, but for now I'd rather you called me Samantha."

"Do you mind telling me why?"

"No. I don't mind telling you. Sam was what my father always called me. Until my brother Joey was born. After that he didn't call me much of anything anymore."

"You were second fiddle then, huh?"

"Yeah, second fiddle in an orchestra of one. Until my mother died. I was real useful to him then."

I reached across to take her hand. She let me. Then she squeezed mine briefly and slipped hers free. "It's okay, honest."

"Sure."

"Let's just sit and listen to the rain awhile, okay?"

"Sure."

So I sat there, sipping whiskey and listening to the rhythmic pattern of the rain. The woman I most wanted to be with sat close enough to touch if she would but let me. All I'd ever wanted was in that room but it was a long way from being mine.

Chapter 14

I AWOKE IN THE SAME CHAIR. IT WAS EARLY AFTERNOON AND MY head still throbbed if I moved too quickly. Samantha had covered me with a blanket. She was gone. A note on the kitchen table said the coffee was ready to be plugged in, wished me good luck and admonished me to be careful with my head.

I dragged in the newspaper and plugged in the coffee. While it was brewing I cleaned myself up and got dressed. I took two aspirin, rolled up a half-dozen more in a Kleenex and dropped them in my jacket pocket. My headache was retreating but not yet gone.

I went into the kitchen and pulled out the folded list Jackie had given me. I hauled down my Yellow Pages and looked up motels. I called one and reserved a room. It would be available at three o'clock. Then I dialed the outcall number.

The phone rang twice and was picked up by a lilting southern drawl. "Garden of Eden Health Salon. May I help you?"

"I hope so, honey. I hear you got an outcall service, girl come out and massage my poor aching body out at my place, that right?"

"That's right, sir. Now if you'd just give us your name and address, we'll dispatch one of our masseuses directly to you." I gave her the address of the motel, my room number and told her my name was Smith, Bob Smith. I shifted into my conspiratorial voice full of halts and stutters with a dash of self-effacement. "Uh, well, you know, I kind of like them—I mean I enjoy it especially if they're, uh, young, you know, real young, uh, you understand. . . ?"

"Yes, sir. All of our masseuses are young and attractive

84

women. We'll see if we can locate one with a particularly pixieish appearance. Our services begin at 120 dollars an hour and escalate depending on your interests. The masseuse has a rate card she can show you."

"And," I continued in a strangled caw, "I like 'em blonde."

"Of course, sir. I'll see what we can do." Ever helpful. I'm sure if I called for an animal act she'd have asked: Guernsey or Holstein, Clydesdale or Morgan, Shepherd or Great Dane.

"Our masseuse should be there in about forty-five minutes. One last thing, sir."

"Yes."

"Will that be cash or charge? We honor VISA, Mastercard, Diners Club, Carte Blanche and American Express."

"Charge."

I called Arnie. While the phone was ringing I looked up Tony Julian. No listing. When Arnie answered I told him I'd made contact. "I made my pitch. Let's see what Uncle Monte comes up with."

"What do you want me to do?"

I gave him the motel address and my room number. "Sit outside in the parking lot and watch the car that drops her off. With a new client the driver will wait for a sign that everything is cool before he leaves. See if you can get a tag number and if it ain't a cab follow the person who drops her off. Especially if it's a guy driving a jacked-up car with a Dixie's Pride sticker, okay?"

"It's done," Arnie said. "Oh, by the way, don't do anything I wouldn't do."

I locked up the house and drove down to the motel. I picked up my key and memorized the layout as I walked back to door number twelve.

Inside, I looked around at the room: two double beds, phone, Bible, color TV, desk, dressers, easy chair, open closet, bathroom with wrapped plastic cups and that absurd wrapper on the toilet seat, signifying god knows what. The ubiquitous standard twentieth-century motel room. In the bathroom I poured myself a glass of water and downed two aspirins. I pulled off my holster and put the .45 under the mattress of the bed on the left. I took out my wallet and removed all the ID and slid that under the same mattress. I sat down in the dark on the easy chair and awaited the girl of my dreams.

In about twenty minutes there was a knock at the door. I got up and crossed the room. I opened the door to an arresting sight. She was petite. Her blonde hair was tied in pony tails with white ribbons, in fact her whole outfit was white. The innocent to be defiled, I was sure. She had on white knee socks and sandals and if it's the shortness of shorts that makes them hot pants these were absolutely incendiary. She was sugar and spice and everything nice, but she was not thirteen. Twenty-three maybe.

"Mr. Smith?" she asked, her hands entwined in front of her as if she were asking for a favor.

"Yeah, I'm Mr. Smith. Come on in." I let her slide past me into the room. She put her purse down on the dresser and turned to look at me, her hands on her hips, her head cocked as she looked me up and down. Boy, I hoped I'd grade out at prime or choice, maybe fetch two bucks a pound. I wondered if she'd kick my tires. She made sure the closet and bathroom were empty.

"Are you a cop or in the employ of any law enforcement agency?"

"No. Hey, what is this? I just want a massage. I mean, that's legal in this state?" I whined.

"Of course, Mr. Smith. I'm just looking out to protect myself. You meet all kinds of unscrupulous people in this line of work." She looked to see if I was satisfied with that and then went on. "Now, our fees are by the service provided. State laws require that the genital areas of both the masseuse and the client be covered at all times, is that understood?" I nodded. "Okay. For the straight body massage using the herbal oils that's 120 bucks an hour. Payable in full in advance. We honor cash, VISA, Mastercard, Diners Club, Carte Blanche, and American Express."

"Uh, I'll pay using VISA." I fished into my wallet for the credit card I have in the name of a dummy corporation. I couldn't believe anyone could recover from this bizarre descendant of the Miranda ruling to muster a decent hard on.

She opened her purse, took out an imprinter, looked at the card, then at me to see if I was a diversified consultant and went to the phone on the desk. She sat and crossed her legs and dialed out. "This is number thirty-seven. Time 3:30 P.M., return call in one hour." She read the card number and the amount. She hung on and flashed a weak smile, but the current was leaking out of it. She patted the bed and motioned me to sit across from her. "Okay, thanks." She ran the card through the imprinter and gave it to me to sign. When I did, she ripped off my copy and returned it to me with my card. She went to her purse and replaced her equipment. Oh, for the good old days of spiked heels and mesh stockings. In the world of commercial sex the emphasis was clearly on commercial. If this got any less erotic I'd pass out. I mean, hookers with WATS line privileges, credit card imprinters and Miranda cards. The road to the perfumed garden was going to be a long one at this rate.

She leaned back against the dresser, flexing her legs and arching her back, "Now, Mr. Smith, of course if you and I succumb to some personal magic and because of that we engage in sexual activities, that is merely a side effect of this encounter between two consenting adults and not the intention of our meeting here."

"Of course." That must have been article two, paragraph B.

"And the fee that I have received for services is in no way connected with any sexual transaction between us. Correct?"

"Right, absolutely." Now I lay me down to sleep.

"Okay." She turned back to her purse and fumbled with something. She went to the window and adjusted the blinds up and down. "The light's pretty bright here," she said. That was her signal to her partner. Then she locked and chained the door. She came over next to me and ran her palms over my chest. She undid the top two buttons and kissed my chest. "Umn, you're a big one." She looked up at me with love or its synthetic substitute in her eyes. "Now, what would you like Mr. Smith? Tell me all about it." Her transmission was clearly in order. We'd just gone from the State Inspection Station to flat out on the highway in one smooth motion.

I looked down at her. She was a good choice, natural blonde, good complexion, faint band of freckles, little pug nose, tiny cleft in the chin, pouty underlip. It was the eyes that were wrong. Not the flat buttons you'd expect of a woman doing her ten thousandth trick. It wasn't the impersonation of desire that a good pro can turn on in the wink of an eye. No, it was something else. The vigilance of a juggler in a crosswind, trying to keep all the balls in the air and find the way out of the wind.

I wondered if I was a ball or the wind?

She picked up on my distraction. "What's the matter, Mr. Smith, cat got your tongue? Here, let me find it for you." She took my face in her hands and kissed me deeply. She pressed her body against mine and as I bent over to be kissed I found myself pulling her against me with my arms tight around her. Our tongues played hide-and-go-seek for a couple of minutes. She won, but then so did I.

She stepped back and said, "I hear you like 'em young and blonde, right, Mr. Smith? Well, am I what the doctor ordered?" She took a deep breath and jutted her breasts out toward me. I found myself in the vertiginous grip of lust and contemplating a very long fall onto her very soft chest. "Yes," I croaked and reached out gently for her breast as if touching a newly hatched chick. I tried to remember that I'd just sworn off falling for long legs and big breasts. I was going under when I threw out a lifeline of words. "What's your name, little girl?"

She looked up at me. "Anything you want to call me, Daddy?" She hadn't moved toward me or away and I looked at my hand on her breast like a toad on a meringue.

"How about Randi?" I searched her eyes. Nothing.

"What do you want your little Randi to do, Daddy?"

I wanted little Randi to go home.

"Uh, take your clothes off real slow, baby, and show me your stuff." Give me a minute to breathe.

She said, "Sure Daddy." and slowly undid the zipper on her shorts and slid them down her pale legs. She slowly turned, then flexed her legs and buttocks and slowly bent over. The Jordache girl run amok. She hooked her fingers in her underpants and slowly peeled them down over her magnificent ass and there it was. Sticking out of her like the fuse to a bomb was the string to a tampon.

"Nice work, sweetheart. I wanted someone young, sweet, virginal and here you are on the rag. That's disgusting!" I shrieked.

She jumped across the room pulling on her pants as if I'd put a branding iron to her. "Jesus man, I'm sorry. If you're so turned off I'll leave." She was pulling her shorts on and backing away from me.

"No way, baby," I said and sprang at her. "Not with my money, you cunt." I grabbed her purse off the dresser. She tried to grab my arm and pull the purse free. I got an arm under her neck and across her chest and with a backhand swipe threw her across the room. She skidded into the closet.

"All right, dammit, that's it. I'm outta here. Give me my purse," she snarled out of the corner.

She started to get up off the floor. I pulled the .45 out from under the mattress. "Just relax and sit back down on the floor, ankles together, your hands around your knees. Pay attention to what I say.

"My name is Leo Haggerty. I'm a private detective, working on a case. I'm looking for a missing juvenile. I think Monte Panczak is running some kiddie action, so I set up this appointment to see if I could get a hook into it by asking for a young girl. You showed up. We do-si-doed for a while, now it's time to talk."

"That's a nice story. Let me see your license if you are who you claim to be."

I flipped the mattress over and found my license and scaled it to her.

She matched pictures and face and said, "So what do you want with me?"

I leaned forward and dropped the gun barrel as a sign of good intentions.

"What I want with you, sugar britches, is everything you know about Monte Panczak's operation and especially Tony Julian. I just bought one hour of your complete and rapt attention, so let's get with it. For starters, have you ever seen this girl or heard her name mentioned. It's Miranda Benson." I took the picture out of my coat pocket and held it out to her.

"No, I've never seen or heard of her."

I stared at her, waiting for her to go on.

"What's to tell? I got hustled by this guy Tony Julian to work in the massage parlor. I figured why not, I needed the bread. He said I had great fingers. What a jerk! Anyway, I told him I wasn't going to do anything but straight massages. Christ, I make thirty bucks for half an hour kneading some drooly doughball. Who needs the sex end to get rich? So I've been there a few weeks now and we got this call for a real young chick and a blonde. I was the only one even remotely like that so Tony came over to me and asked if I wanted it. He said it was a straight request. I could make of it what I wanted."

"If you don't trick what was all the hot and heavy with me, then?"

"I didn't want you to get really pissed off and call the service. One of the girls said to wear the tampon because it usually turns off the guys who want the 'little girl' scene."

"How long have you been there, to the day?"

"Three weeks and two days."

"And you haven't tricked once?"

"No."

"What are you up to?"

"What do you mean, what am I up to?"

"Just what I said. Nobody works massage and outcall for three plus weeks without turning a trick. The pressure to produce is too great. You're up to something. Let me tell you that if I'm wondering about it, you can bet that Monte's thinking about it, and when he decides he knows what you're up to he's going to put you in the foundation of his new tennis court."

She said nothing.

"Good, you sit there and think about it. I don't know who you think you're playing with but you are in over your head."

We sat and stared at each other for a while.

"Okay. I'm a reporter."

"A what?" I'd have been less surprised if she'd said she was a Martian.

"A reporter. I'm doing a story on the outcall massage business and thought that a new angle would be to tell the story from the inside. The stories of the girls who work in these places."

"You are major fucking nuts, lady. Do you know that?"

"Why?" she said indignantly.

"Why? I'll tell you why. You're doing a story? What's this great story going to do? Stop prostitution? Not bloody likely. Get Panczak busted? No. I can see it now. I have to protect my sources, your honor. If the story ever sees the light of day it might get you an award. Whoopee! If Panczak finds out what you're up to, you are fucking history. Who knows what you're doing? Anyone?"

"My editor."

"Wonderful. Wonder-fucking-ful. If I was you I'd make plans to wrap this story up real soon. You aren't in deep cover, you're in deep shit."

"Thanks for the concern," she said sarcastically.

"Think nothing of it." I'm sure she didn't. "What can you tell me about Monte's setup?"

"He runs it like a business. When they hire you, you sign a contract saying you will not use the organization to further your own prurient interests or engage in illegal sexual behavior and that you indemnify them against liability for your actions. Then they tell you what gynecologist to go to if you suffer an occupational injury. Can you imagine a workman's comp claim for pregnancy or the clap?"

I didn't want to tell her that the injuries they had in mind were from the "freak" tricks, the sadists. I'd had a bellyful of that on my last case.

"Any mention of using underage girls?"

"No. I've never heard any of the girls mention anything like that."

"Do you know anything about Julian? Where he lives? He may be hiding this girl somewhere."

"No, but I'll keep my eyes open. Let me see that picture again. I want to be sure I'll recognize her if I see her."

I gave her the picture and one of my cards. "Call me if you see or hear anything, anytime." She put the card in her purse. "Don't carry them around with you. Memorize the face and my number and destroy them. I'm not kidding."

"I hear you. I'm not stupid. I've done this kind of work before."

She sat on the bed and called in to the service to let them know that everything was fine and she needed to be picked up.

"If you ever have to do this again, just tell the guy your herpes has flared up. Nobody's going to strip search you to see if you're lying."

She turned away and had the doorknob in her grasp when I said, "By the way, what's your name, so I can recognize the byline?"

"The name's Johnson. Terri Johnson."

I reached under the mattress and retrieved my shoulder holster and the rest of my IDs. I dropped the IDs in my coat pocket, shucked the jacket and slipped the holster on. In the mirror I saw Terri Johnson standing in the doorway watching me. She left and I waited for Arnie to return.

I called Mr. Benson at the work number he gave me. His secretary answered. "Benson Construction Company."

"Mr. Benson, please."

"He's not in. May I take a message?"

"That's okay. I'll call back." Something jabbed at me from my memory but I couldn't grasp it.

My thoughts drifted to Samantha out on the streets. A frail bag of flesh and blood walking around that can be taken from me in an instant and there may be nothing I can do about it.

Maybe that's the deal I've made with myself: I'd rather be lonely than helpless? Maybe I'd rather not.

Arnie arrived a couple of hours later. I crossed the room and asked who it was. He said, "Little Bo Peep" and I let him in.

"Interesting trip, Leo. It was Julian and some big spade with him. I know I've seen that guy somewhere before. Real big mother—six foot eight inches or so, about 300 pounds—looked like the Trans America Building on wheels. He moved pretty good. Bullet head, goatee, wraparound shades, lots of bright shinys. Anyone you know?" I nodded no. "Definitely muscle. If brains were dynamite he didn't look like he could blow his nose. They went from here to a building down on the docks in Olde Towne. Right near the Interarms warehouses. Picked up a couple of boxes marked Film and went out to a little house out near Lorton. Very interesting place. A run-down building that sits on a plateau above the road. Lots of open fields. Woods in the back. Brand new barbed wire fence all the way around. Brand new gate at the driveway with a real good lock. All hooked up to an alarm system. A lot of money for an old shack. He went downstairs in the house, pulled some shades across the windows at the ground level, stayed a couple of minutes and left. Then he went back to the massage parlor. Later on a couple of guys showed up in a van, parked it out back of the parlor and went upstairs. They left after a few minutes carrying one of the boxes. Guess what was in the van?"

"Snow White and the Seven Dwarfs?"

"No. Only one dwarf. Nosey. A lot of very expensive camera equipment, lights and so on. Well, these guys left and then Godzilla and Julian went out to eat. I came back here."

"Looks like something's coming together and I don't think it's the Cannes Film Festival."

I looked at Arnie sitting on the bed. "Let's get out of here. I didn't like myself here."

Chapter 15

WE LEFT THE MOTEL AND DROVE TO ARNIE'S HOUSE. IT'S A bungalow similar to mine. What the real estate people call a "starter home" for the newlyweds. Except that in the baby's room was a vast collection of weapons from around the world: American handguns; rifles; shotguns; knives; English Calthrops; the Bag'hnak of India, a weapon so fearsome that its mere possession was punishable by death; blowguns from Borneo; German crossbows; Japanese long swords and the kusari-gama or sickle and chain. The house is always well lit and the shades are never up.

We pulled up silently to the house with the lights out. Arnie surveyed the outside and then proceeded to disarm the front door. We went in and threw our coats over the living room chairs. I checked the time: 6:45. Arnie went into the kitchen to get something to drink. The house was barely furnished. I wandered into the armory, by far the most interesting room. On Arnie's bulletin board was a single page of paper. It said: Way of the Ronin: Late 20th Century. Below were eight lines:

(1) Approach all things without memory or desire: The truth lies between.
(2) Take care in all matters; the least may be the most and this is not given to us to know.
(3) Readiness is all and is the fruit of diligent practice.
(4) Knowledge of many things is the sword unseen.
(5) Above all know one's self and that of one's enemies.
(6) Be discreet in all matters; a *ninja* of your desires.
(7) Do not make enemies, let them create themselves.

(8) In the symphony of life a player of all parts will not be silenced.

I looked up as I felt Arnie's presence. I was uncomfortable and felt like a spy. He handed me a glass of Jameson's on the rocks.

"What's this, Arnie?" Casual as bird shit I was.

"It is what it says it is. It's what I've learned in the last ten years."

"I've never seen it before."

"I've just begun to work on it. It seems the right time."

I looked back at the list and slowly read each line. "Hell of a path to tread."

"It's the only one that makes any sense to me."

"What is a *ronin* anyway?"

"They were the masterless warriors, the samurai who were set loose after the rise of the shogunate. Those who could not reorient themselves after the social order they were embedded in had dissolved were a scourge upon the land." I had never heard Arnie say this much about his past or his thoughts. He seemed uncomfortable with it.

Arnie turned and walked out of the room. I followed, wondering where in the process Arnie was or wanted to be. We went back to the living room. It was past seven. I called the service. There was only one message. Terri Johnson had called and left her number. I copied it down, hung up and then called her.

It rang three times. Terri picked it up on the fourth ring.

"Hello."

"Terri Johnson?"

"Yes."

"Leo Haggerty, returning your call."

"Yeah, right. I had another call to go out on after I left you. I tried the herpes routine and it worked. Okay, long story short. When I went back to the club I talked to Tony. I told him I had a john with a yen for young girls and that I didn't turn him on.

95

That he wanted the real thing. Tony said he could get me a movie of a girl—young, blonde, doing it—to show here at the house to turn him on. Said it would be dynamite stuff. Anyway, he said it'd be ready in a few days and he'd let me know. He told me to keep it to myself, that Panczak wasn't to know about it. Tony wants to be a big deal himself. So I asked him if I could see it and he said I could see them make it if I was nice to him. Christ, he acted like he was taking me to Disney World! He said they're going to shoot it tomorrow morning, around nine out at a house near Lorton. He's going to take me out there himself."

"Thanks. We'll see what we can do. There's a big black guy with Julian. Is he going to be out there?"

"Yeah, Leroy. He'll be there. He's in charge of keeping the peace."

"Leroy. What's his last name?"

"Dixon, I think. Why?"

I snickered. "Shit. He was a college all-star with a big mouth who couldn't cut it in the NFL and here he is enforcer for a vice emperor. I love it, it's perfect. Listen, we've cased the place. I think the shooting room is below ground. We need to get down there easily. Can you make an opening for us? Let the movie get rolling, everybody'll be occupied, then excuse yourself. Tell them you need a little air. We'll keep your cover intact but we'll come back in behind you and get the drop on them. I know what I'm asking you to do, so if you say no, it's no problem. We'll just do it another way."

There was a long silence between us.

"I'll do it. They've been eyeing me since I got back to the salon. They may be getting suspicious like you said. I ought to do something to make it look like I'm serious about this outcall stuff. And anyway if they are using this girl, I want to be a part of stopping it."

"Listen, thanks. Hang loose when it happens. It could get very nasty. Dixon's a wacko and I've got a guy with me who makes him look like Pope Pius XII."

"Okay, just be sure to get the girl out, will you?" It was both query and plea.

"We will. I've got to get to work."

"Bye."

"What's our first move?" Arnie said.

"I call Panczak and clear it with him. I don't want him thinking he was ripped off and that he needs to set an example. We get Julian and Dixon out from under him and nobody'll give a shit what happens to them."

"Then what?"

"We stake out the Lorton house overnight, so we're there when they arrive. I always like to be early to things. You avoid a lot of setups that way. Then wait for our moment and do our thing. Just like I told Terri. When she gives us an opening we take it."

I picked up the phone and got Panczak's number from information.

"Hello."

"Monte Panczak, please."

"Who's calling?"

"None of your business. Just get Panczak."

"Fuck you." He hung up. I dialed again.

"Listen, asshole. Somebody's setting Panczak up for a fall. If he finds out that he's in the house of many doors because you didn't put this call through you won't be able to run far enough. Now get him." The line was open but silent.

"Yeah. Who is this?"

"This Monte Panczak?"

"Yeah. Who're you?"

"Not important. Just consider me a friend. You've got some disloyal employees, Monte. They're running a little action on the side. High risk stuff. The kind they could take a nasty tumble for. Maybe get turned around, plea bargain your ass away."

"How do you know all this?"

"They've got something of mine. I want it back."

"So what do you want with me?"

"Just to let you know that I'll be moving against these people and that it has nothing to do with you. I just want what's mine. What you do afterward with them is up to you. I thought you might appreciate the warning. I'll be handing them to you on a platter. You can go in and clear it up right away. No expensive outside talent needed to do the work. The boys in New York never have to know. Just sit tight and keep your ears open. You won't be able to miss it. What do you say?"

Panczak was silent a while, then said, "I'll give you forty-eight hours to get back what you want. Then I clean house. When I clean house I don't give anything away. What I don't keep I burn. If you're too close when I set the fire that's your problem. You got forty-eight hours from now. And, friend, you'd best not be fuckin' with me. I've got a short fuse and a long memory."

We began to prepare for our camping trip. Arnie called the weather to get the temperature, chance of rain and sky conditions. Then he looked up the moon's status. We each made up a packing list. Arnie dressed quickly and then assembled the items on his list: ski masks, surgical gloves, his mummy bag, a good shovel, a sawed-off Remington 870 with magazine extension. Then we went to my house. I dressed and then packed a Thermos, trail mix and jerky, some wire cutters, my mummy bag, binoculars and a roll of Day-Glo tape. We were dressed all in flat black: black wrestling shoes, black wool socks, black cotton pants, black turtleneck sweaters. I felt the Colt .45 under my arm and thought: Yea though I walk through the valley of the shadow of death I will fear no evil because I'm armed to the teeth, goddammit. I slipped my Gerber knife into the small of my back and put the Beretta Jetfire on my ankle. Arnie wore a belt with a flat black clasp. He moved to adjust it and then in a single sweeping motion the clasp was off and a four-inch dagger extended from a ring over his two middle fingers. We took no wallets, only cash taped to our ankles.

As we were walking out of my house I asked him, "What's the weather gonna be?"

"Clear skies, no moon, zero percent chance of rain, slight wind East South East, temperature overnight upper fifties, tomorrow eighties. Perfect. God is smiling. Good night for a mission. Just like old times. Let's go."

I locked up and went to Arnie's old Chevelle, got into it and we headed into the night.

Chapter 16

WE DROVE IN SILENCE FOR A WHILE. HIS LAST COMMENT MADE me think of Vietman. A place I'd never been to and one Arnie had never entirely left. I balanced the impulse to talk with my wish to defer to his silence. He was sorting through larger ruins than I. Finally he spoke as we got to an unlit intersection.

"That's the road there. It runs alongside the woods above the house. If we go east we can catch Hooes Road into Springfield or we can go west onto Ox Road into Burke. We'll need to disable their car before we go in so we don't need to worry about pursuit."

I nodded. He was in his element.

We cruised slowly down the road from one end to the other. Arnie and I memorizing its twists and turns. Arnie found a place where the woods were thinnest and we parked off on the side of the road and emptied out our gear and left the car unlocked. We hiked down into the woods to where we had a clear view of the house. It was the first rule of terrain: take the high ground.

Arnie said, "Let's dig in and set up."

We quickly dug two shallow holes to sleep in, put our bags in them along with guns, wire cutters and the shovel and covered them with leaves and dirt. We hung the food bag from a nearby tree. Arnie put strips of Day-Glo tape on a string of trees from the fence to the road. We went down to the fence and inspected it.

"We'll cut it when they disarm it. Then run a dummy wire around to complete the circuit. I'll make the hole wide enough for two to go through at once. If you're dragging the kid, you won't have to carry her through."

"Fine."

"After we get ready to go down, we clean up our gear and put it by a marked tree. I'll get it on the way back if I can. I don't want to lose that shit if I don't have to." He shrugged. "And anyway leaving materiel behind is lousy form."

Arnie and I went back up the hills and slipped into our sleeping bags. As I spread the dirt and leaves over me, I thought, if this doesn't work out this could be my grave I'm lying in. I folded my arms across my chest with my .45 in my left hand. As I lay there I thought of Colonel Colt's lullaby: "When danger threatens fear no man of any size, just call on me and I will equalize." I didn't sleep any better.

"We'll sleep in four hour shifts, okay?"

We lay in silence for a while. I was supposed to sleep first, but I couldn't. "Arnie, whatcha thinking about?"

"I'm thinking it's been over ten years since I lay down in a hole in the ground and thought about killing somebody."

"Yeah, well, it's a first for me," I said.

We got quiet again. The wind moved slowly through the trees, rustling the leaves. Every now and then a bird called out. I looked up at the stars. The night was cool, the air crisp, the sky clear, only I was muddled. I smelled the dirt and leaves on my chest, a faint scent of rot. Now I lay me down to sleep. I should be on a blanket with Samantha, I thought, celebrating life and love.

I'd used Arnie's talents a number of times since I'd met him but we had never talked about where he'd learned them. Vietnam had long sufficed as a one word answer. There was an unspoken regard between us, perhaps friendship, perhaps not. The official party line was that Arnie had skills I could use and I provided occasions for him to hone those skills. I suspected that we avoided talking about the war because the gap between warrior and protestor threatened our fragile alliance. I decided that I could no longer simply use his skills without at least being willing to hear how he'd learned them and at what price. Maybe he didn't care if I knew or what I thought. Maybe there was no common ground possible between those who went and those who did not. I had to know.

"What was it like for you over there?" I asked.

"What's to say? War is hell, plain and simple."

"Why'd you go?"

"Oh, I knew I couldn't go to jail. I'd have gone crazy being locked up and I guess I just couldn't imagine life in Canada forever. Christ, I was only eighteen. I guess I thought one year in Nam and I'd be free. Canada was exile forever. Ain't that a kick in the ass. Believe me, if I'd had a better imagination I'd have taken Canada."

"Where'd you serve?"

"Up country. I was a Green Beret—"

"You don't sound like you were gung-ho. How'd you become a Green Beret?"

"I was gung-ho on staying alive, that's why I became a Green Beret. I was scared shitless I was gonna die, so I wanted to be the best goddamned soldier possible so I'd live and they'd die. If I was gonna go over, I was gonna come back."

"I wasn't there." Officially I fucked up my knee playing ball so I was 4-F. But my "Toronto in Springtime" brochures were well thumbed before I donated my ligaments to the alumni association.

"I know. When I told you I'd been in Nam you never asked what unit I served in and when. That's the first thing another Vet wants to know: where were you and when were you there."

I knew I wanted to ask Arnie more. It was like interrogating the survivor of any disaster asking, "What was it like? How do you go on living now?" Part of me felt like a leech. What I really wanted to know was that I'd been right not to go. That it wasn't simply cowardice. Maybe that's what the last ten years on the streets had been about.

"Is that list you had on your wall part of what you went through?"

"Yeah. It's taken years to start to sort it out. The war sure didn't make any sense. Man, we took the same ground so many times your boot prints wouldn't even be gone before we'd step in them again. So many guys died for nothing. That'll take the heart right out of you. You just turn everything off inside. You know fuck everything. I wasn't very good at that. Buddies are buddies. So I started reading samurai stuff, trying to figure out how they did it. It helped, gave me a direction. In war be a warrior; everything else is bullshit. It got me through."

"I knew I couldn't go. It just seemed like a stupid place to die. Stupid reasons to die for."

"Most of them are. I sure wouldn't die for God, Country or the American Way anymore. Love or money, maybe." He laughed bitterly.

"Did the killing get any easier there?"

"Yeah. If the first one doesn't drive you crazy it gets easier. Pretty soon it ain't anything at all. That's the other reason for the stuff on the wall."

"How so?"

"When I came back everyone hated us. 'Baby-killers.' Shit! Everybody I killed was trying to kill me. If he was fourteen, go talk to his mother, not me. Anyway I could feel myself getting angry all the time. So I withdrew even further, trying to control myself. I wasn't going to be some psycho people could point their fingers at: 'Mad Dog' Kendall. I went through too much over there to piss away my life like that. If everybody was gonna hate me, fuck 'em. So long as I don't hate myself. That's what the code is for. So I don't lose myself even when everybody else is lying to me." Arnie stopped and then began again, his voice lower and softer. "That's the one thing I thank God for. I did some bad things but I never did anything I hated myself for. And that, brother, is a lot to ask for in hell."

I thought about the hell of unatonable guilt. A cloak the wearer weaves into the very fabric of his being. A prison of one's own devise. A pain without respite.

"Shit, man, let's get some sleep. All this bullshit won't change what happens in that room."

I looked up at the stars, the constellations, the North Star. How much harder to navigate that inner space of desire, wish and need.

I fell asleep in a swirl of doubt about what I'd kill for. Death is the last editor, there are no revisions allowed. You'd best be damned certain about what you submit to that reading.

Chapter 17

ARNIE WOKE ME AT FOUR. I STRETCHED AND FLEXED MY ARMS and legs and back to make sure everything was working, took a deep lungful of air and asked him how the night had gone.

"No movement in the woods; you can hear the traffic up on the road. Some kids wanted to park up there but saw our car and moved on. A car just came by and stopped. I didn't hear anybody get out but we ought to check the car to see if it's been tagged as abandoned. If so we'll have to move it and relocate our stuff."

"Okay. Get some shut-eye. I'll check it out." My eyes had adjusted to the light. I unzipped the bag and then brushed back the earth, stopping after each action to listen to the silence. It remained unbroken. I rolled out of the ground, did a push-up to get the blood moving and moved off at a forty-five-degree angle from our site toward the road. Despite the absence of moonlight there was reasonably good visibility. Every few steps, varying the number, I stopped. There was no shadow I could detect. I crouched in the woods twenty feet down from the car. There was no yellow tag on the door. So far so good. I reversed my path and five minutes later was once again enfolded by Mother Earth.

I spent the next four hours listening to Arnie snore, wondering how he lasted one night in the jungle, making that kind of racket. The cars moved up and down the road. I listened to the legitimate residents greet the day. At eight I whispered a sweet nothing in Arnie's ear and one eyelid rolled back, like a crocodile. He regarded me with reptilian calm. He arose as I did. Within a few minutes our gear was packed, the earth tamped down, leaves spread around and we were moving down to the fence. At the edge of the woods we squatted, checked our weapons once again, reviewed the plan, ate some jerky and trail mix and washed our mouths with water. Today was not the day to have a full bladder. An hour later a black and gold car pulled up to the front gate. Arnie slid down to the fence. I watched a big black man get out and put a key in the gate lock, turn it, and push the gate open. "Now."

Arnie unwound the wire, attached the metal clips to the fence and then cut out a four-foot section. As soon as the car was through the gate the black guy got out and rearmed the fence. We'd just made it. You could hear the juice hum through the dummy circuit.

Arnie came back to where I was sitting. I screwed the lens hoods on the binoculars and could make out Leroy Dixon and Terri Johnson. I put the glasses down. Something dark rippled under the suface of my mind and vanished. I picked up the glasses and watched Dixon swing the car around so it was pointing downhill, get out and go around to let Terri out. He pulled her out of the car and walked her to the door. Except for the tape across her mouth everything looked just fine.

"Shit man! Something's gone wrong here," I said as I turned to Arnie. He pressed his finger to his lips and then pointed upward. I handed him the glasses and he left. I watched him climb a nearby tree, go up about twenty feet and then lie down along a branch and survey the terrain. All he needed was a tail to flick off the flies. He descended quietly to the ground, squatted, brushed away the dirt in front of him and diagrammed our situation. He pointed at me and drew a line from us to the car, our marked trees. He held up four fingers, made his hand into a gun and located the men on the ground. Two trailers: one on each side of our path, fairly close together. Two front men, wider apart. The idea was simple enough. The front men were to contain us. Either flush us into the open field or back into the trailers. I was right, we had dug our own graves. Now we had to keep from filling them. Arnie pointed to me and moved his fingers to the east in a big semicircle behind one of the trailers, cupped his hand under his chin and mimed a cut throat. My lips tightened and my stomach rolled as the adrenaline rushed in. He then drew a second car on the road—theirs—and moved me into a place midway between one of the lead men and the car and motioned palms down for me to hold that position. I pointed to him and then the map: Where would he be? He put his palm on the ground and simply wiped everything away. Our eyes locked for a moment. He gave me the thumbs-up sign and we moved out. There was nothing to say. I couldn't imagine we would die. The thought is paralyzing and that is halfway dead. There would be time to talk later.

I crawled down along the edge of the woods a good fifty yards, stopped, looked back into the woods, saw nothing and heard nothing. I slowly began to pick my way through the woods, ass down and eyes open, stopping randomly to check for sounds. Nothing. These guys weren't half bad but that'll get you all dead. I scurried and stopped, zigged and zagged like a mouse across a linoleum floor. Just keep moving. If you're still moving, you aren't dead yet.

Adrenaline time had set in. Everything was in slow motion. The blow that hits you seems to take forever to arrive. As the blood shoots out the first reaction is surprise. How could I not have gotten out of the way? Then shock sets in and there are no other thoughts. I had moved midway up to the road. Arnie hadn't said our car was out of action. Dixon's arrogance or their bad timing was going to cost them. He knew we were up there and he didn't care if we saw him muscle Terri into the house. He must have figured we weren't going to be telling anyone. They had us outnumbered and we'd left them a Day-Glo path to find us. But they were late or cocky and we were still alive in the woods. I wished I'd been a Boy Scout. I was a little short on wilderness skills. They had come up here to kill us and there was nowhere to run to or any way to get there. I lay down and waited. I pressed my ear to the cool earth to see if I could feel their footsteps. Nothing. I sat back up. Time passed, then I heard liquid rhythmically slapping the ground. You dumb schmuck, I thought. To lose your life because you couldn't hold your water.

I located the guy, maybe a dozen feet in front of me. His back was to me, both hands occupied. Black, youngish, wiry, dark clothes. Hopefully his gun was in his waistband. I slipped the knife from the small of my back and got a firm grip on it. My knees were still debating with me, but I'd never have a better moment. It was time to cross the border. He'd kill me if he got the chance. I bunched my legs under me, held the knife tightly and uncoiled across the ground at him. I slapped my hand across his mouth and drove the blade deep into his throat and ripped it across like I was opening a letter not a man. His life ended in a sheet of crimson rain. He died so quickly that I fell over on top of him from my own momentum. I wiped off the knife and rolled away from him. My arm had been pinned under him and as I drew it out his head turned to face me. He stared at me. Brown-eyed, stubble-cheeked, a young black man without any future at all. Blood still ran from his mouth. I wanted it to stop. He was just a boy. Who would send him on such a job? What kind of child would go? I wanted him to be the last child to die. I rolled back and began to pat him down. I rolled him over, pulled the gun out of his waistband and tried not to look at his flaccid penis, dangling uselessly before him. I went through his pockets and got a ring of keys, some coins and some pills wrapped in foil. Other than the gun he was clean. I rolled him back face down. I didn't want him to be embarrassed when they found him. Then I slithered into the brush.

I lay in the brush and realized I could hear my heart roaring in my ears. There was no time to stay. The war was still on. I tried to get my bearings and sighted a marked tree. The dead man was ten feet off it. I drew a line from the tree through his body and off into the woods and began to scurry backwards along it. I was placing myself between the other men and their car. I lay down on my stomach and pulled out my .45 and his .38 and lay very still. There were still four other men walking around these woods, armed, looking to kill each other. We were chess pieces come to life with death the only mate. I tried to imagine the thoughts of the three men hunting us. Assuming surprise, and knowing they outnumber us, they'd hurry to finish the job. They'd been moving in a funnel to force us into the open or back into a cross fire. When they got to the edge of the woods, began to curve back and found the funnel was empty, what would they think? They couldn't call out to each other. They'd wonder if we were on the run or hunting them. Assume the worst: that you're being hunted now. You still outnumber them. If you find the dead kid you know somebody's behind you, between you and escape. What do you do? Do you try to run and get out? No. The people you were hunting have shown you they'll kill. They're not likely to let you leave. So you have to fight your way out. What do you do? Be cautious. Compared to Arnie I was a novice at this sort of thing. On this chess board I'm a pawn and he's a queen. A wild piece moving through the woods, knocking off the other pieces. Unless they've got a queen too—or two or three. So it's time to sit and wait.

I put back my .45 and checked the boy's gun. A Smith and Wesson, a reliable piece, not a Saturday night special. I tried to get comfortable, shaking and wriggling myself like a snake shedding its skin and lay there trying to be as receptive as possible. Sight and sound. Distal receptors. Early warning. Keep your screen clean. No ruminations, regrets or wishes. Those are the prerogative of the victor and the day was not yet done. I put the .38 in my left hand, loosely held but ready. I didn't want to be cramped up when they came. I lay there and waited and I wished the fucking birds would shut up. If you lie in the woods and listen, it's as noisy as the New Jersey Turnpike. It's just not human noise. I took off my watch and put it in my shirt pocket; I had the rest of my life to wait here. For a long time I merely listened. My eyes defocused. I followed each bird's sound as if they were notes in a song. Plotted them as a series of lights on a screen in my mind's eye, incorporating each chirp and tweet into a harmonious pattern, waiting for the sound that would not fit. And so I waited but slowly my reception grew bad. The signals were unclear. The fuzz of fatigue was taking over. Noise became signal. I shifted channels and began to scan the woods, brushing each bush and clump of tangled underbrush with my eyes. Back and forth, left to right. Then my gaze moved up and over as if I were spraying these woods with pesticide. Nothing. I began to think about the interplay of motion and vision. If the eyeball is kept still and the visual field has no movement, the receptors fire and then there is just whiteness. We see at all largely because of our restless eyes.

I wondered if I could lie still enough to let the world whiteout until someone out there created movement and then track them. Let them reveal themselves rather than searching for them.

It didn't work. I didn't think it would. I squeezed my eyes closed. Then open. Then saucer-wide to start all over. Maybe become a radio again? I felt the tension in my body. The muscular message was that what I didn't know about would hurt me—in fact it would kill me. I lay there. Be patient. I thought what if everybody crawled off and left and I just lay here until they put the new highway through? I'll just gather myself up, apologize to everybody and go home. Wouldn't want to be late for supper.

How long would I wait here? Maybe a rabbit will go down a hole nearby and I'll just follow him out of this mad wood.

I'd wait until dark. Then if I'm not found, I'd try to make my way out. Until then I'll play this as Arnie said: wait for him to flush them to me. If it doesn't happen by dark Arnie will probably be dead. So I wait. I lay there starting to gear up into another round of the Sparrow's Symphony when I heard a sound. "Leo, it's me, Arnie. Don't move. Don't say anything. I'm coming out into the open." He stepped out of the woods into a clearing not twenty feet from me. I started to rise but didn't. What if he'd been captured and used to flush me out?

He moved into an opening directly in front of me. I scanned the woods to either side, looking for a gun barrel covering him. Nothing. A man could be directly behind him. I waited. I knew he wouldn't betray me. Didn't I? It wouldn't buy him anything. I waited to see how he would play it.

"They're all dead, Leo. It's time to go home." Silence. "Good. If I was you I'd want proof too. Here." Slowly he lifted up his right arm. In his hand was a severed left ear. He dropped it, "one," he raised his arm again, "two," and again, "three." Three ears for the matador. No tail this time. "You left your guy facedown in the woods with his dong hanging out. That makes four."

I slowly let the air out of my chest and relaxed my grip on the .38. Thank god it was over. I pushed off the dirt and stood up in front of Arnie.

"Jesus man, what a fucking horror show. Is that what it was like? The silence? The waiting? The unknown?"

"You got it. You sit in the jungle and people drop all over the fucking place without a sound and you don't know who's out there—friend or foe—or where he is. Makes you real patient and real careful. One other thing. Next time you do a throat, lift up the chin first. Getting yourself pinned down by a corpse can make you one yourself."

"How do you know that?"

"I was twenty feet off your flank killing the guy who was stalking you."

Arnie reached into his pocket. "Anyway, here's their car keys. Let's get the fuck out of here. I've gathered up all of our gear and obliterated our setup. These guys didn't have any IDs on them, so it'll take a while to make them. There's just four bodies in the woods. It'll take a while to figure out what happened. I killed each one a different way. That should muddy it up a little. Let's go."

I started to turn away, a little befuddled that four men were dead in those woods without a sound. I wanted to go back and see each one to make it real. It felt like one moment of stunning reality in a moving hallucination. "No, we can't go. Terri's still down in that house. We've got to get her."

"Man, there's nothing down there to get. They let us see her because we were all supposed to die up here. She's dead. Let's be gone."

"No, she's down there because I asked her to help us. It's on my head. I've got to check. You go load the car. Meet me at the front gate. All right?" I handed him the boy's gun.

Arnie sighed, shook his head ruefully and then took the key.

With no need to worry about revealing my position I picked my way quickly through the woods and stood at the edge of the field. Shading my eyes, I looked down at the house. Dixon's car was gone. I jogged through the grass to the house, coming up from the left side where there were no windows. I crouched by the side of the house, pulled out my gun and peered around the corner. The ground-level windows Arnie told me about were all curtained. The main floor windows were all shuttered. I took a deep breath and listened for any sounds. Three times nothing is nothing. I crept across the front of the house, stepped up on the porch and touched the knob. It rolled easily in my palm and I was in the house. The upstairs was empty. I could see three rooms: bedroom, kitchen, parlor, all empty. All dark, hot and closed. A resort for mushrooms.

I went down the short central hall toward the kitchen. On the right was the cellar door. The padlock on it hung open in the hasp. The door opened out. I gripped the knob in my right hand, stood out of the doorway and slowly pulled it open. Nothing. It was pitch-black down that staircase. Anyone down there would know I was at the top of the stairs. I reached back, took the lock off the door and rolled it down the wooden stairs. I followed it down and pulled the door closed. It drew no reply. I squatted on the stairs, letting my eyes adjust to the dark, my ears to the silence. The room opened up to my right. I could make out klieg lights, a bed, camera mounts, a circle of chairs, a toilet and sink without a door, a clothes rack on one wall, a small table with bottles on it. The whole room was open to me and it looked empty. Gun in hand, I crabbed down the stairs. On the opposite wall were the light switches. There was a foul smell in the room.

I thought of just turning about and leaving, but perhaps Leroy had done something stupid, like left a map of where he was going.

I flicked the switch. She was there on the bed on her back. "Jesus Christ." I shuddered. She had not died easily. I holstered my gun and walked over to the body. I grabbed a sheet off the floor to cover her with. As I spread it out and began to pull it up over her I turned to look at her one last time. I wanted to remember what Leroy had done when I came to render the bill.

"Help me, please help me," she whispered. Her eyes danced and bulged as if they were trying to fly from her face.

I crouched next to her. "Terri, it's okay. This is Leo Haggerty. It's all over. It's gonna be okay." It's gonna be okay. What the fuck was I talking about?

"I can't move. I can't feel anything. Oh god, I thought I was going to die here."

I leaned forward, her eyes focused on my face and I asked her what happened. As I did that I reached down with my left hand and took a firm pinch on the back of her forearm and squeezed hard. Her eyes never left my face. She stopped and licked her lips. I told her to wait, I would get a towel and wet her lips. I found one on the back of the toilet and put an end under the tap.

"He raped me."

"Listen, I'm just going to wet your lips. Don't try to swallow any, you might choke." I patted her lips and brushed her face, pushing back the tendrils of her hair from her forehead.

She took a deep breath. "When he was finishing he said he was going to fuck me to death. He grabbed my neck in his hands and started to twist my head around. I heard my neck break. When I came to I was alone in the dark. My throat hurt too much to scream. I tried to get up to run but I couldn't move. I was so scared. I thought I was going to die here, alone, slowly." Tears began to well up in the corners of her eyes.

"Did Leroy say anything to you. Any clue to where he'd be going from here?"

"No. He just laughed and said there was no one to save me. That you'd be dead too."

"Did he say anything else, anything at all about his plans?"

"Yeah." She furrowed her brow. "He said killing people was going to solve all his problems and then he said that I was just a tune-up. That the real McCoy would make him rich."

I went back to the sink and moistened the towel. I brought it back to Terri and carefully wiped her face.

"What happened? How did they find out about you?"

She took a painful swallow. "The next trick I went to was a plant. When I didn't trick he must have called them back about me. They wanted to know who I had talked to. They burned me with cigarettes. The film thing was a setup to flush you out. Leroy told me they've been ripping off Panczak for months. They thought that I was spying on them for him. They were going to kill me and you to keep it quiet."

"All right. Now listen to me. I'm going to have to leave you. I'm going to call the cops and get an ambulance here right away. I can't move you and we need to get you to a hospital. Okay?"

"Will you come right back, please? Don't leave me here."

"Terri, I can't. He's still got that girl and he's going to kill her. The cops will be here in minutes. They'll be here before I even get back." I stopped talking and wondered if a victim on hand is worth two in your mind. "I'm going to try to make you more comfortable for when they come to get you." I went and got two bolsters off the floor and gently put one of each side of her head, next to her swollen, bruised neck. Leroy's handiwork was impressed into her flesh, a necklace of death. I put her arms down at her side. Before I put her legs together, I took the towel and cleaned her. She had messed herself when she had gone into shock. The fact that she would have twitched spastically, evacuated and gone white when she went into shock probably convinced Leroy she was dead. Fortunately he had broken her neck too low, leaving her alive. Fortunate was my word, it was not my life. I pulled the sheet up over her legs.

She was trying to speak. I bent down to hear her. "You know I didn't want to tell him. I'm sorry."

I pulled the sheet up over her burned breasts. "Yeah, I know you didn't. It's okay.

"I'm going to leave the doors open upstairs so you can hear them when they come in. They'll be here in five minutes Terri, just hold on." She whispered okay and I left. I wedged a towel under the door at the top of the stairs and then latched open the front door to the house. I stood on the front porch scanning the vista for a sign of Arnie. Every time I tried to think about Terri entombed in her own flesh my thoughts dissolved into a blur of horror. It was too much. Too much. I tried to focus on her, to keep an image of her in my mind, force it into my furnace of rage and make it a weapon, but I couldn't. One thought did come clearly to me, as insistent as a pulse: my fault, my fault.

Arnie pulled up the road in his car. When he pulled around in a circle and I didn't move, he looked at me. I stepped off the porch.

"Let's get to a phone, man, and in a hurry."

"What's up?"

"What's up is that Terri Johnson is down there with a broken neck, paralyzed from the neck down and we're gonna get an ambulance out here fast. Let's go."

"We've got one thing to do first though," he said.

"What's that?"

"Drop me back at these guys' car. I'm going to take it over to Springfield Mall and leave it on the lot. It'll be months before it's noticed. You get the ambulance and pick me up on the lot."

"Fine."

Arnie gunned the motor and we slewed down the driveway out onto the road, then left toward Hooes Road and Springfield. As we turned onto Hooes I noted the road to the house, Lorton Church Road. I dropped Arnie at the car and flew up the road. On the right was the Springfield Volunteer Fire Department with an ambulance. I spun into their lot, jumped out and ran into the glass-fronted dispatcher's office.

The dispatcher was sitting at his desk, deep into solitaire. He looked up, furrowed his brow and squeezed a yeah around the dead cigar lying in his mouth like a downed telephone pole.

"I've got an emergency. There's a woman with a broken neck in the basement of a house—the first house on the right on Lorton Church Road. She's paralyzed from the neck down. Listen, can I use your phone? I need to call the police." He pointed to a phone on the desk opposite him, flipped a bank of switches and began to bark into the intercom system. I plugged my ears and dialed the phone number.

"Fairfax County Police. May I help you?"

"Yeah. Please get me Lieutenant Schaefer." I never tell people it's an emergency unless there's no other way to get through. Everybody has rules for how to react to the word "emergency" and they do things their way, no matter what. "Emergency" doesn't speed things up; it delivers you into the deepest part of institutional bureaucracy where the rules are the most rigid. Everybody's so busy covering their ass with cast-iron Pampers that nobody cares to hear what your trouble is until they're sure it won't jump up and bite them. So you do it their way or not at all.

"Schaefer here."

"Frank, this is Leo Haggerty. I'm at the Springfield VFD. There's a woman, a reporter named Terri Johnson, in the basement of a house out there with a broken neck courtesy of Leroy Dixon. I'm here getting an ambulance for her. Dixon's driving a late model black and gold Caddy—a Seville, I think. The only places we've seen him are a building down in Olde Towne, near the Interarms warehouses and that massage parlor on Washington—The Garden of Eden Health Salon."

"Is Johnson dead, Leo?"

"No, Frank, but she might wish she was. She's dead from the neck down."

"What the hell is this all about, Leo? What the fuck is she doing out in Lorton? And how do you know all this?"

"Listen, Frank, I'm going after Dixon right now."

"Bullshit, Leo, you stay put and out of this. Whatever's going on stinks and it sounds like it's fucked up eight ways to Christmas. I don't want anything else fucked up. I'll send men to those places. You come in to talk, now, or I'll have you brought in."

"Sorry, no can do, Frank. I'll explain later." I hung up and sprinted to the car. An ambulance was already on its way, heralded by its nasal siren's whine.

Three minutes later I picked Arnie up on the Loisdale Road side of the mall.

"Now what?" he said.

"We find Dixon and the kid before he kills her." I sat quietly, trying to put together what I knew so far in a way that would tell me where Dixon would go. My anxiety kept intruding, tumbling my thoughts. It was like trying to read Plato on a high wire.

"Pull over for a second, Arnie." We slid into a MacDonald's parking lot. I squeezed my eyes shut and put my head in my hands. Killing solves all problems. Terri was a tune-up? Big money and the real thing? Killing Terri and me might keep him out of jail or clear of Panczak for a while but his days are numbered. He couldn't keep dipping into the till forever. Why kill the kid? If she's willing, he can just set up elsewhere. Maybe she's not. Maybe she's become a liability. He'd want one last big score so he could clear out. Tune-up? Sex and death a tune-up? Sex and Death and Big Money? I was sick when it made sense to me.

"Let's go to Olde Towne, Arnie." We swung out of the parking lot and went up the ramp to 395 North and then hard right across four lanes to the 95 North ramp heading to Alexandria. Six minutes later at a discreet sixty-five we were in Alexandria. We turned right on King Street and headed into Olde Towne. It's the section between Washington Street, the road to George's home and the Potomac. Bounded by the disenfranchised on the north and the "truly needy" on the south. Olde Towne is just that. There's Washington's church and Robert E. Lee's childhood home. Plaques on most of the buildings attest to their being part of the original "Olde Towne" area, circa 1749. It has cobbled streets and an architectural dress code. No golden arches here. It's also the boutique and restaurant center of the town and the air is full of the minty fresh smell of new money. Traffic creeps by, since parking places are scarcer than a black face in this end of town. It's Virginia's answer to Georgetown—mankind passing in close quarters lubricated by good manners.

We drove down King Street, the central spine of this section, all the way to the river. Then right past the Interarms warehouses. We turned right at Union Street and saw no Alexandria Police Department cars on the street. Maybe we were too late and it was all wrapped up and done. Maybe Fairfax and Alexandria were squabbling over jurisdiction and no one had arrived yet. We went down Union Street between the rows of numbered weapons warehouses to another red brick cube, three stories high. We pulled down the alley between it and Interarms number seven, toward Water Street and there it was: a black and gold caddy snuggled up behind the building.

Chapter 18

ARNIE PULLED DOWN THE ALLEY TO WATER STREET. WE WERE AT the southern end. A straight run of four blocks up to King Street then a left and the city would branch out before us.

"I don't like being in a corner at all." Arnie shook his head.

"I want to be able to get out of here in a hurry. I don't want Leroy chasing us on the streets after we fuck up his car. I don't think he has any backup for this shtick. Panczak gave us his blessing, remember."

"Yeah, but what about his buyer?"

"Buyers are rodents, ferrets. They stay low and in the dark. Sunlight kills them, you don't need bullets. Okay?"

Arnie shrugged. If it really stank he wouldn't do it, not for me or anybody. "You know we stick out like sore thumbs in these outfits. Who the hell dresses like this for a stroll in Olde Towne."

"We'll split up then. Together we look like a sandwich board for a mortician."

Arnie pulled two windbreakers out of the back seat and we pulled them on over our shoulder holsters. He handed me a pair of surgical gloves. I slipped them on, flexing my fingers so that they fit snugly. Arnie did the same. I patted the gun and the knife in the small of my back. "Okay, I'll go up the alley. You go up King Street and over on Union. I'll kill the car and go up the fire escape and work my way down from the roof. You start at the bottom and work your way up. Okay?"

Arnie nodded. "Fine, we'll do it that way. I'll start up the ladder a few minutes after you. The two of us together are as inconspicuous as a varicose vein on a Rockette."

Arnie headed off toward King Street and I walked up the

alley, staying in the cover of the high fence around the Interarms warehouse. At the junction of the two alleyways, I looked up at the back of the building. Three fire doors connected to the escape ladder. Two windows on each floor, one on each side of the door. First floor: curtains; second floor, shutters; third floor, blinds. I looked both ways before I crossed, just like my mother taught me, and glided across the alley to Leroy's wheels. As I pivoted around it I felt the hood for engine heat. Still warm. He didn't come here right from the farm house. He dropped off the girl or picked up somebody else and got here not too long ago.

I squatted down alongside the car next to the wall, pulled out my knife and stabbed the front and rear tires. The car slowly listed into the pavement. I sheathed my blade, grabbed the bottom of the ladder and pulled it down. As soon as it swung down I pulled out my .45 and moved as smoothly and quietly up the ladder as I could, stopping every flight to check for noises. As I got off at the third floor I looked down and saw Arnie approaching the building. I pulled on the fire door and when it opened thanked the great fire chief in the sky. The door closed and I hugged the wall. I let my eyes adjust to the darkness, my ears to the background sounds, trying to filter out the sounds that pipes and floors make from those that people do. Nothing.

The building was old. The fire escape was added on to a building with only an elevator on the inside. It had been built back in the good old days, before people realized that elevators don't work during fires and that for the people trapped inside them they become giant casseroles. The hallway went the length of the building then flared out into a foyer. The elevators were there. There were two doors on this corridor and one facing me on the far wall of the foyer. Maybe three offices. I wished we'd just stuck our noses in and looked at the directory in the foyer first. But then we might have bought it right there. I edged down the hall to the foyer and learned nothing. The door on my left said Please Enter around the Corner. The door on my right said Orthodontic Laboratory. There was a fire extinguisher on the wall. I took it down and pulled out the safety pin and left it on my right side facing the fire escape where I could grab it on the way out. I edged up to the foyer. The elevator was to my right. Opposite me was a door for an insurance agency. Just above the knob a newly lettered sign proclaimed We Also Prepare Tax Forms. The hall continued on after a jog to the left leaving a dark corner beyond scrutiny. To my immediate left was a door marked Ace Film Company: Processing, Sales and Distribution. Bingo.

I slid along the wall and grasped the knob, slowly turning it and then pushing it inward. I pulled out my Colt and went through the door in a crouch, scuttling sideways. If there was an alarm I'd have company soon. Two minutes alone gave me my answer. The front door was for show and whatever inspectors needed to be paid off. There was a desk for a a receptionist and behind that another door. In the back would be a storage area for the films they distributed and sold and processing equipment for their own film. The major centers for making adult films for theater releases are New York, Los Angeles and San Francisco. If Monte was making his own, and the setup at Lorton sure pointed to that, they would be eight millimeter loops for the peep shows he owned around Fort Belvoir. I sat a moment and heard voices from the back. I crossed to the secretary's desk and found the alarm button on her desk. In case of a raid she'd hit that button. It would be a silent signal and anything unsavory would be quickly destroyed. The side door I'd passed in the corridor would probably be for an exit off the boss' office. I figured a corridor beyond this first door with his office to the left. Then processing equipment and a storeroom in the back. My guess was that Monte's office would have equipment for "screen testing" his stars and for private shows, and that's where they'd be.

It was time to find out if my mental map was worth a damn. I crouched by the door and pushed it inward and repeated my crab imitation going through. So far I was right. Over the door there was an alarm light which was not on. It would have been visible from anywhere in the room. In the right corner was a vault holding the films they kept in stock. In the left corner was a darkroom, but the door was open. Around it was other processing materials and equipment. There was an office off the corridor as I expected. I went through the door to his office. The voices were coming from the den. The furnishings were early pimp with unlimited bucks; rococo excess. Scarlet shag rugs, black leather, not vinyl, chairs. Side bar with cut crystal decanters, large rosewood desk. Behind that a throne where the prince would hold court, twirl his ruby ring and grant wishes. Paneling, genuine I'm sure, on the walls. Indirect lighting on wretched art. Furnishings are for comfort and pimps are connoisseurs of that. Art is not and they are lost with it. The left hand wall had an aquarium except the fish were dead. The plants were all plastic. Behind the desk was the hall door. To the right, the door to the den. I moved in the disjointed slink of the stalking cat to the door and listened to the voices.

"Tony, I don't want to do this. I don't like him. He gives me the creeps."

"Shit. Goddamn it. Shut up. Listen, all you gotta do is this last one, for Christ sakes and we'll be set. Leroy's got somebody lined up who'll pay a lot of money for this flick. We'll be set. We can split and go to California if you want, anywhere." I listened to Tony mesmerize her. First the staccato crackling of a live wire. Then slowly the sentences got longer, slower and he began to turn the world upside down. Randi was so lost she'd follow anybody who offered a direction, believe any tour guide. If you love me fuck this stranger. Earth to Randi, come in please. There was silence. She was thinking. Maybe.

"Just this last one? Promise me, Tony? No more. Then we'll go away, just you and me, and have a good time, okay?"

"Yeah, this is the last one, kid. I promise you."

"Oh thank you, Tony. I'm so happy," she cooed. "I'll be good, I promise. I'll do a good job. You'll be proud of me."

This shit had gone on long enough. I leaned back from the door to open it when my head was smashed back into it. Stunned, I was pulled back and saw the tomato stain from my nose on the door before I was rammed into it again. The roof got low and I was shrinking into a pinpoint. I lost my body from below my teeth. I spun on a crazy arc upward into a wild blooming flower of electricity that lit me all up and I spent forever falling down.

I returned from the circus in my skull, all blinking lights and clanging gongs, to find myself tied with amateur enthusiasm to a chair. As the world coalesced into light and shadow, then shape and color, sound was added. Finally I slowed into the same time zone and made sense of it.

There was a bed before me and a bank of bright lights. Off to one side was a movable camera frame with lights above it and sound equipment on the base. Leroy was in front of the bed thrusting himself rhythmically forward. As he turned to keep his best side to the camera, I saw his hand ram a fist full of blonde hair into his crotch like he was unplugging a toilet. His eyes were closed and his brow furrowed. He was getting ready to come. Leroy reached down and twisted her nipple like he was trying to tune in a radio. The head stopped bobbing and Leroy cursed at her. "Suck it, bitch, before I kill you."

"That's what you're gonna do anyway, Leroy, right. Fuck her and kill her." Ice picks went through my head and I had to close my eyes.

Leroy's head spun around. "Hey, the badass white boy is back with us."

"What's she worth to you, Leroy? Twenty-five thousand for the master? But you'll keep a copy, won't you? Any time you need money, just make a print. She's worth more to you dead than alive. Dying on film like that she'll last forever. Killing her is like an investment, huh, Leroy. Thinking of your old age? You want something to retire on, huh? Didn't last long enough with the big boys to get retirement pay, did you." I didn't know how long I could keep it up but I wanted Randi to know what was going on and to try to get out. Leroy was gonna kill me one way or the other.

Randi was backing up on the bed on all fours, shaking her head from side to side and starting a low moan. Sick and frightened she was looking for a wall to melt through. A way to not be. Unfortunately, this play has no intermissions. If you come in, you sit through to the end. Leroy zipped up his fly and grinned at me like I was a side of ribs with slaw. "Well, if anybody's going be dying it gonna be you, white boy."

Randi was backed up against the bed frame, her hands to her face. Her mouth was open silently imploring Tony to tell her this was just a bad dream and they'd still go away together and have a good time. Tony just stared at everyone.

Leroy started to walk toward me and I prepared to hurt.

"Whoa there, super nigger, the cavalry has arrived." Arnie stood in the doorway, his .45 aimed at Leroy's chest. He glided into the room and shook a knife into his palm. Keeping his gun on the group, he bent down to cut the ropes.

"Now, *kemo sabe*, about that raise."

"Shit, man, just get me out of here." As the ropes fell away I brushed them off like spider webbing and tried to stand up. My head was throbbing. I sat back down and hoped the concussion was minor. Head injuries are no joke. One too many and you can wake up a member of the plant kingdom.

"Tony, Tony, what's happening?" Randi began to keen. She reached for him. Tony moved from around the corner of the camera frame toward her.

"Randi, no! He's in this too!" I yelled but too late. I felt like a safe on wheels had slammed up against my eyes. Julian had pulled her in front of him and put a knife to her throat.

"All right, don't anybody move. I'm going right out the door. Anybody moves and she dies." He pointed to me. "Pick up that nightgown and throw it to me." I did. He draped it in front of Randi and limped with her as his dead leg to the door. As soon as he was through he pulled it behind him.

I looked at Arnie and at Leroy.

"Go get her back. She's the one that counts." Arnie nodded.

Arnie picked up my gun from a nearby table and slapped the Colt into my hand. He looked at me intently. "Are you okay? Can you handle this?"

"I'm okay. Go get the kid."

Arnie backed out the door and pulled it behind him. I pointed the gun at Leroy. "Sit down, shithead. You ain't goin' anywhere." Leroy sat.

I clenched my teeth and was breathing through my nose. My head hurt like hell. I tried to slow down my breathing to keep myself as still as possible. Maybe the big heavy thing with all the points would stop rolling around in my head. It was getting worse. The floor was tilting up at me. I was determined not to black out. Let's keep everything simple. We only have to do two things: keep our eyes open and our gun up. Arnie'll be back in a flash. Right. I stretched my eyelids and forced them wide open. Got to conserve energy. Shut down everything but my eyes and my hand. My eyes were okay. Eyelids up, captain. My gun began to droop. I jerked it up. Sweet Jesus! My head exploded. I righted myself and drew a bead on Leroy.

He looked back at me and chuckled. "You one stupid mothafucker. Why you care so much 'bout these cunts? That other blonde mama yours? She wouldn't tell me about you at first. I had to hurt her real good." He chuckled again. "Couldn't get her to shut up then. Stupid bitch."

"Shut up. Dammit." I knew what he was up to. Get me listening to his voice. Thinking about what he was saying. Distract me enough so I couldn't keep my eyes open.

"Know what she said when she was begging?"

"Shut up." I screamed. The top of my head flew off.

"You know I got her to move her ass real good when I was doin' her. Made her tell me how much she liked it. She ever tell you that?"

I was on my feet, bug-eyed and grimacing. Rage purified me.

One wish. One deed. From the bottom of my heart I was going to blow his fuckin' head off.

I was on my knees. My eyes were going different ways. I put my hands out in front of me. I was going to throw up. I looked up. There he was! Those hands. Those damn hands! I shoved my gun into his smile. A giant wave rolled me over. I'd never seen a purple and yellow snowstorm before. I had to rest. I was so tired. Just a minute. I promise. I'll be fine.

Chapter 19

SOMEBODY TOOK THE COMFORTER OFF ME. IT WAS TOO HEAVY TO wear in summertime. I felt better after my nap. Arnie's face loomed over me. "Goddamn. I knew I should have crippled that fucker. Are you okay?"

"Yeah. My head is killing me. Where's Leroy? Did he get away?"

"Yeah. All the way to forever."

I slowly moved my head. He was lying next to me. One of his headlights was out and most of his control room was gone. I was getting sick again. I rolled away and slowly got upright.

Arnie went out the door and came back dragging Randi with him. He was tight-lipped and tense. She was sullen. "Let go of me, you bastard."

"Shut up, shithead, before I lose my temper."

"And what, hard guy?"

I looked quizzically at Arnie. "Trouble communicating?"

"Fuck, no. This bitch communicates fine. She just doesn't know what's good for her."

Randi continued to wriggle against his hand on her arm. I took a moment to look at her. Her blonde hair was tangled. Her face was transformed by her sullen vermillion pout and glaring black-rimmed eyes from child to ageless bitch. She was slim, firm and beginning to ripen. Past buds but the fruit was not yet full. Long legs, short torso. She was on her way to womanhood. I wasn't sure if that would be a blessing or a curse or whether she'd ever look or feel like a child again.

"Where's Tony?" I asked.

Arnie smiled. "Tony had an accident. He fell in the stairwell. I fucked up the elevator when I got here and then foamed the staircase with the fire extinguisher you set out. He took a header going down and bounced a flight or so. What took me so long was getting some rope to tie him up with, and this bitch." He shook his head at Randi. "She acted like we were the bad guys. I was tempted to leave her with the jerk. She tried to bite me while I dragged her up here. I told her she'd eat baby food for a month if she didn't cut that shit. All she seems to understand is threats."

"All right, let's get out of here. The police are going to be here soon and I'd just as soon not have to explain you to them."

"What about Tony?" Her voice was a whine.

"Oh, good old Tony. Good old Tony arranged with good old Leroy to kill you on screen for the eternal delight of necrophiles everywhere. Do you understand? He sold you out for money. He was going to let Leroy fuck you and then kill you on film. It was going to be your last film for sure. Your last anything. So much for good old Tony. Let's get out of here."

I went to the camera, yanked out the film and stuffed it inside my jacket. Then we each grabbed an arm and hustled her out the door.

As we were going out of the building we stopped at Julian, tied up in the stairwell. I asked Randi, "Anything you want to tell him?"

She looked down at him. He started to turn his face away. Arnie rudely realigned him with his foot. "I loved you. How could you do this to me? What did I ever do to you?" Julian looked at her without remorse, contrition or comprehension, just annoyance at having to explain himself.

I squatted down in front of him and got his attention along with a fistful of his jewelry. "We don't have time for you to think about this yourself so repeat after me, douche bag: 'You never did anything to deserve it. It was all my fault. I never loved you. I just used you to make me feel good.'" Julian lay there dumbly. I banged his head to remind him. "Say it." He responded well to

128

that. "I'd ask you to tell her you're sorry but you've lied to her enough. Let's go, school's out."

We got to the bottom of the stairs. Arnie looked at us. "This won't fly. Two guys in black pajamas with a nymphet in a baby doll bathrobe. No way. Olde Towne isn't ready for this."

"Okay, you go get the car. We'll go out the back way and meet you in the alley. Say one block up at Interarms."

Arnie sidled out the door and we went down the corridor to the back door and out into the alley. I looked both ways and seeing no one began to steer her up the alleyway to the next warehouse, keeping close to the walls. At Interarms we ducked into a walkway leading to a loading office to wait for Arnie. Randi had been quite subdued since we'd left the building.

She looked up at me. "Where are you taking me?"

"We're taking you out of this nightmare. Everything is going to be okay. As soon as we can get to a phone I'm going to call your father to pick you up."

Randi wrenched herself away from me wailing, "no no" and tried to fling herself into the roadway. I grabbed her about the waist from behind and pulled her back toward me. Arnie better get here soon or I'm going to be shot as a rapist. I spun her around to me and said, "What's the matter?"

The acid rain of her tears tracked her face and ran through her harlequin's cheeks. She looked up at me and said, "Who do you think started me?"

Chapter 20

JESUS CHRIST, I THOUGHT, IS THERE A BOTTOM TO THIS MESS?

Arnie pulled up into the alleyway. I looked at Randi. "I won't take you to your dad, okay? I don't know exactly what to do for you, but I'm going to try to get some help."

I don't know what she read on my face but she slid into the car. I followed and slammed the door. "Let's go to my place, Arnie. I have some calls to make." He put it in gear and we left Olde Towne behind, the sound of sirens filling our ears. We went up Duke Street out of the historic section, through the boarded up gutted section, to Telegraph Road. We snaked around the ramps onto the beltway heading west. My mind was ineptly active, churning out thoughts in incomplete pieces, unable to catch any of them to study. All my trains of thought were in the round house. I took a short look at Randi, sitting between us, eyes front, mouth somber, her hands folded in her lap like she was going to church or the doctor's. A painful business but "for your own good." Her nightgown was staggeringly inadequate and I reached into the back seat and got Arnie's rough army blanket to cover her. She thanked me silently and arranged the blanket over her legs and around her body, tucking it in and holding it down with her arms. I looked at Arnie, contemplating the road. I wondered just what all this meant to him and his code. Was he reviewing how he handled himself? Did he care about what happened to this kid?

We pulled off the ramp at Gallows Road and turned down toward my home. It's a bungalow I'd bought with a big finder's fee I'd gotten six years ago before mortgages became the prerogative solely of the very wealthy. Arnie coasted into the driveway. I slid out and as Randi got out with me I told Arnie to stay by his phone. This wasn't done yet.

I walked up the slate path to the door, unlocked it, turned off the alarms, went in and turned on a foyer light. Randi stood in the doorway looking in.

"Listen, if you want to stay out there, that's fine; just let me get you some clothes. I'm going to call a woman I know to come out and stay with you while I try to figure out what to do. You can come in and sit by the door if you want and even keep the door open, okay?"

She pulled open the door, took the chair I scooted over to her and sat in it.

"All right, I'm going to get you some clothes to put on; they won't fit but they'll cover you." I felt like I was trying to talk a strange dog out of disliking me: I'm going to walk away slowly now, like this, okay, big fellah? I went back down the hall, alert to any sound of the front door opening, went to my bedroom and got her a pair of my running shorts and a T-shirt to wear. When I returned she was still there. Remarkable. I handed her the clothes. "If you want to shower and get cleaned up, the bathroom's in the back, off the master bedroom. You can change there. I'm going to call my friend, okay?" She just sat there dumbly watching me. A gulf of caution lay between us that words would never cross. I decided to give up. If she trusted me that was nice. If I could help her that was better. I went into the kitchen to the phone, picked it up and dialed Samantha. No answer.

I turned back to Randi. She was gone. I looked out the front window to the street and sprinted to the front door. As I flung it open I heard the shower turn on and I smiled ruefully.

I went back to the kitchen and dialed another number.

"Law Offices. May I help you?" was crooned into my ear.

"Walter O'Neil, please." Formal.

"May I say who's calling?" Solicitously.

"Leo Haggerty." Silence. I ran some tap water while I was

waiting and downed two aspirin. My head was pounding like high tide in the Bay of Fundy.

"Hello, Leo. What can I do for you." Walter O'Neil was my lawyer and friend and very capable at both those things.

"I've got a little problem, Walt, and I'd like some advice."

"Okay, shoot."

"I've got a girl here with me now, a runaway I picked up for her parents. She was involved with some real heavy weight assholes in the kiddie porn ring. I bailed her out of that and now I find out she claims that her father was the first one to have sex with her."

"My advice, Leo, is very simple. Turn it over to Protective Services and walk away from it. These cases are absolute hell and they'll make you crazy."

"How so?"

"They're almost unprosecutable, and even when they are, sex offenders almost never serve time in Virginia. Instead they get therapy which as far as I can tell doesn't often change anything. Mostly it's the kids who get the short end. They get shunted around to foster homes. They're ostracized by the family. If they go to court they're assaulted on the stand by the defense attorney. The court system is not set up to deal with children as witnesses. Drop it. Believe me."

"Humor me, Walt. Why are these cases such problems? Send me to school."

"Okay. Take your kid—how old is she."

"Thirteen."

"Super. How badly was she beaten?"

"What do you mean?"

"Thirteen is the rubicon in sexual offenses. Under thirteen you'd best not touch a child. Over that coercion is required and the state likes to see physical evidence for that."

"But she's his kid. He didn't have to beat her up. Don't they understand how the promise of love can get them to do themselves in?"

"Sorry, Leo, but Virginia isn't ready for such a radical notion.

If the child consents your case is ninety percent shot to hell. Listen, in fact in Virginia the child can be charged with incest as well as the parent. How's that for a bite?" Walt lowered his voice to somewhere deep in Dixie and drawled "Yer honor this po' God-fearing man was seduced by that wanton hussy. That shameless wench who confused his po' fatherly instincts with her ripe young body and preyed upon his love for her. Hasn't this man suffered enough, I say, to know that his child would use him so?" Don't laugh, man, I've seen it done here, especially if the girl is at all attractive."

"Well, what charges are available to her?"

"Thirteen and without force, not much. Just crap like indecent liberties, contributing to the delinquency of a minor, indecent exposure. People get sent to the mental health centers on charges like that. Too damned often they go for a while, all the time resisting changing, just complying with the court order until the therapist gets fed up and writes a report with some crap on it like 'patient has reached maximum benefit of treatment; recommend to be terminated' which the judges sign and the guy walks. Maximum benefit, shit. All that means is 'therapist is too tired of fucking around with this jerk who has no interest in being here other than to get court off his back. Respectfully submit you do so, so I can help someone who wants it.'"

"That's it, then?"

"No, but other problems exist. If there was oral or anal sex you can charge the person with sodomy, but if the child consented and was thirteen—bad luck, that number—you can also charge the child. Or you can try for statutory rape because she's under fifteen but with that there are tremendous evidentiary problems. When you said the kid had been making porn flicks that just adds problems. Any aspect of the child's sexual history is admissible if it provides an alternative explanation for physical evidence of sex. You haven't got a lot to work with. She's of the age where coercion needs to be shown and you haven't any visible scars to show. Her own behavior contaminates the physical evidence that her father had sex with her. I'm sure there are no witnesses to these sexual encounters. It boils down to pitting the kid against her father and let me tell you if the father plays hardball that can be an incredibly ugly business. 'Would you care to tell the jury, Snow White, just how it felt when you were sucking your daddy's cock? Did you like it?' I wouldn't want to put a kid through that, knowing the uncertainty of justice in the courts without a signed confession and eight-by-ten-inch glossies of him with a gun at her head."

I had no problem at all imagining Mr. Benson in the scenarios Walt had described. "Excuse me, professor, but exactly what did happen to justice?"

"Justice," he scoffed, "nobody wants justice, Leo. Victims want vengeance, villains want mercy. Justice lies somewhere between and it's of interest only to the state, not the participants. Don't expect it to be anything else or you'll be mighty disappointed."

"Christ on a crutch! Who needs the law!" I snapped.

"We need it, Leo, my boy. Our law is primarily designed to protect us from the state as a threat, not from each other. The significance of that fact seems lost on our native white citizenry. Try to imagine the whole fucking state as the enemy, not some isolated wazoos—now that's a nightmare. Leo, do what I suggest: walk away from it. Class dismissed."

"Thanks, Walt. Send me a bill."

"Fuck you too, friend."

I put the phone down. Randi was in the doorway. She had on a pair of my long khaki slacks rolled up like pedal pushers and my T-shirt pulled up on her waist and knotted in front. "The shorts were too big so I put these on 'cause they had a belt. Is that okay?"

"Sure." What am I going to do with this kid? We'll go one step at a time, I thought. I can't send her home and the law's as much a harm as help.

She'd washed her hair and wrapped it in a towel. Her face was clean but she looked worn and tired.

Let's start with something basic. "Would you like something to eat? I'm not much of a cook but it won't kill you and it'll stick to your ribs."

"Yeah. I'm starving." She sat down at the table, eyeing me from a distance. We were proceeding with caution.

I went to the refrigerator and squatted before it, surveying the leftovers and never-beens, creating combinations in my mind and then discarding them. I opted for basic peasant. I took out three potatoes and a package of ground beef. I went to the sink and began to wash the potatoes. I looked over my shoulder at Randi still staring at my back.

"Would you please set the table? The plates are there above the dishwasher. The silverware's here by the sink and the glasses up there." I waved around the room, pointing to closed drawers like a circus barker telling of unseen wonders.

Randi sat the obligatory long count before she pushed off from the table to begin to set it. I went back to the potatoes. I finished washing them, and got the Cuisinart out, put in the shredder and pushed them down the feed tube. I put them to one side.

"Where are the napkins?" Her voice startled me.

"Oh, in the pantry over there." I pointed and she pursued.

I set up two skillets, turned on the gas and melted the butter in each one. In one I placed the shredded potatoes. I took the meat out and made two hamburgers, gently wrapping the meat around an ice cube. I turned up the heat and put them into the pan.

"We'll be ready to eat soon. What do you want to drink?"

No reply. I turned. Randi was staring out across the lawn. Some kids were walking down the street. School was out and the bus had just dropped them off. They walked in close groups, some of both boys and girls, some not, the groups talking animatedly with an endless tossing of hair and book-clutching giggling. The stragglers walked alone and were silent. I looked from the kids to Randi and back. What she saw and felt I didn't know.

She put her head down on the table and made a terrible noise.

It began low and broke into a wail, a windstorm of sorrow rushing up out of some place long ago locked off inside her. The sound peaked and then fell away to racking sobs. She held her stomach and rocked. The food burned and smoked. I turned it off. I wanted to stroke her, to hold her and console her, to lie to her. I didn't want her to be afraid anymore, to hurt anymore, to be afraid of me. I looked at my hands, thick, square, useless.

I couldn't stand that sound. I had to stop it. I sat down next to her and gingerly put an arm around her shoulder. She was so far down into herself she didn't even know I was there. I held her tighter, an island in the storm, a way back. She leaned against me and I began to rock with her, back and forth, the oldest comfort there is. Rhythmic warmth surrounding you, the first consolation for being born. Small, cold and alone, your heart beating wildly you slowly attune to the mother's rhythm, her enfolding calm. Slowly the sobs began to slow down in harmony with our rocking and we rocked more slowly. I undid a piece of the towel on her head and brushed her tears. She took it from me, unwound it from her head and rubbed her face, trying to erase the tears as she would a stain on a stone. Tears are a poor salve but they're all we've got.

I sat back and looked at her. She met my eyes clearly and directly. Defiance and entreaty swirled in her face. Now or never.

"For me to help you I need to know something about what's happened to you. Will you talk about it?"

She nodded yes.

"What happened with your father?"

She bit her lower lip, looked down at the table across all the years of her life and with a deep sigh let her secret go like a black bird. "When I was little he would come to my room when I was in bed and tuck me in and give me a kiss good night. Well, he started to touch me and asked me to touch him and I did. He told me it was our secret and not to tell Mommy. She'd be angry. I was afraid but I felt special and he let me do all kinds of things so I felt he loved me. He told me how pretty I was all the time.

That's all I wanted was for him to love me." She paused at hearing what she'd said. "Anyway, one day I asked him for a puppy and he said yes, I could have a puppy. My friend Jennifer's dog had had a bunch. They were so cute. So I got the dog. I named it Brandy. You know Randi and Brandy. Only I had to be nice to him. He wanted me to, you know, put it in my mouth." The memory passed through her and she shuddered. "It was terrible and I wanted to stop but he got very angry and said he'd put Brandy to sleep. I was so afraid that I just let him do what he wanted."

"What about your mother—did you tell her?"

"I tried once. I told her I didn't like him tucking me in at night. I made up something like I didn't like the way his beard felt when he kissed me good night. She just got angry and told me he was my father and I should respect and listen to him and be thankful that he cared enough to tuck me in at night. Lots of girls never got that from their fathers." She stopped to catch her breath. She looked like she was running from her own words.

"So it went on like that. I would just lay there and let him do it when he wanted to. If I said I didn't want to he'd get so angry he frightened me and I was too afraid to run away then. Anyway, pretty soon he wanted to, you know, do it all and I said no more. He did it once and it really hurt. I lay in bed as long as I could but then I went to the bathroom. It hurt so bad I wanted to see what had happened to me. I sat on the toilet. I was bleeding and I didn't know how to stop it. I was shaking and started to cry for my mother. Anyhow, she came in and saw me holding myself and bleeding and said that there was nothing to be upset about. It was normal and it meant that now I was a woman. She gave me some Tampax to put in myself and said we'd talk about it in the morning. I thought I was going crazy that night. That somehow this was normal and she knew all about it and it was okay."

She licked her lips and asked for something to drink. I offered milk or juice. She wanted a beer. We agreed on ice water.

"I walked around school in a daze. I couldn't believe that was how you got to be a woman. I tried to imagine Jennifer's father doing it to her or my other friends. Anyway, one day I decided to ask Jennifer if her father had made her a woman yet and she looked at me like I was a Martian or something. She said that was a disgusting idea and where'd I come up with such a creepy thought. God, I felt so stupid and so alone."

"This was after you stopped seeing your friends at school?"

"Yeah, I was so weird and different, you know, but I couldn't tell anyone. So I just spent more time by myself."

"Why did you decide to run away?"

"I told my father I didn't want to do it anymore and he really surprised me. He didn't get angry or anything, just told me not to tell my mother and we'd just forget all about it. I said fine, I didn't care about anything but that it was over. Anyway, I found out about why he let it end so easily." She shook her head and the tears began to well up in her eyes. She squinted to shut out the pain that twisted her face into a grimace. The sobs began to jerk her up and down: a puppet pulled by strings attached at cruel places. Her words came through the tears anyway. "I saw him coming out of Tammy's room one night just like he used to do with me. I was so scared. I ran in there and talked to her. It was just like with me—first the touching. I was so angry I wanted to kill him, so the next day after he went to work I came back from the bus stop and told my mother what had happened. Boy, what a mistake. She went crazy, called me a whore and a slut and how could I be so evil as to say that about my father and what kind of woman did I think she was and I was sick and needed help and she was going to call a psychiatrist for me. I just freaked out completely and ran out of the house and got a ride to the mall. I was hoping Angie would go there after school to hang out. I was so mixed up."

"How'd you get mixed up with Tony Julian?"

"He was cute and said he, you know, liked me a lot and anyway he had his own car and place, and I was really afraid. I had no place to go. I had nothing, no money. So I went with him. He was nice to me, he gave me some money and got me something to eat and talked to me. He seemed real interested, you know, said he wanted to help." I hoped the parallels weren't lost on her. "So I stayed with him. He was nice and let me do anything I wanted. I slept late the next day and we just bummed around, you know, bought some records I liked and some clothes, I didn't have any. We ate out. He just seemed to like me and let me, you know, be myself. He had lots of dope and we got high and that made me feel better. I'd never done that before. Boy, was I missing something. I didn't feel so alone or so scared anymore. I thought about going to school and my friends but I just felt so weird around them, not around Tony, so I didn't go back to school. We just hung out and had a good time."

"How'd you get involved with Dixon and that scene?"

She shook her head in dismay but not disbelief. "That night we were back at his place and we'd gotten high again and he came over to me and wanted to fuck me and I could see it happening all over again. All I could think about was what my mother had said to me—I was a whore, a slut. So I said, if I'm a whore, be a whore—who cares anyway? It didn't surprise me that that's what he wanted and he treated me okay, so why not? What's the big deal? I was pretty high. That made it better, you know, like doing it but not really. Like it's not you that's doing it. So I just lay there. At least it didn't hurt and he was done pretty fast. I just decided it wasn't that terrible and he seemed to treat me okay, you know, let me do what I wanted, and made me feel good sometimes so why not, at least he wasn't my father, you know. I didn't feel so great the next day, you know, kinda crappy like I was bad and that's why this was happening to me. I kept trying to remember Jennifer and thought about talking to her but I knew I was getting weirder every day. So I just got high and it all went away. Sometimes I'd feel so bad I wanted to die. Like I was never gonna be okay again and then other times I'd just say to hell with it, you know, fuck it." She eyed me to see my reaction to her story. I don't know what she saw. She went on. "Who cares? So when they wanted to take pictures of me and Tony doing it I didn't care. After you've done it with dad, what's left? Right?"

Of all the things she lost, her sense of horror might have been the most important. Without it there's no way to say no.

"So I did it, I got high. It was kind of a gas, you know, being bad like that. Everybody got off on it, you know what a super chick I was to do it and how sexy and I could be a star and I turned everyone on. I felt like sending one to my father to blow his mind. It felt good, you know, everybody said I was awesome, you know special."

"Do you want to go back to that?"

She fixed me with a stare as if I were the Martian now. "What else is there? It's what I seem to wind up in." She stopped and thought about it for a while. "No, not really. Tony was just like my dad. Always angry if I didn't want to do what he said. You know what I'd really like to do? Make so much money I'd never have to do anything anybody tells me, just be by myself."

I thought about what had happened to her and what she wanted for herself. I wondered if there was any way to get there from here. A plan began to take form. It was far from perfect but it seemed like the least awful alternative.

"Let me tell you what we can do." She looked straight at me and pulled her legs up under her. Sitting on her feet, she began to nibble her thumb nail. A child's posture, dependent, yet strangely provocative in her. She seemed to exude an aura of passivity and compliance that was intoxicating. She'd better learn to protect herself. She was a walking invitation to abuse. Take care of me, be kind to me, and I'll let you do anything. The world did not lack for men who would embellish her invitation with rococo designs of their own. If your father will what else should you expect?

"I can try to get you a second chance to be a kid. I can't undo what happened to you. What I can do is clear a space for you to take a look at yourself, who you want to be. The world isn't just your father and Tony Julian. There're people out there who can love you and take care of you. The world is also full of people who will use you and ball you up and throw you away when they're done. But only if you let them. If you don't want that then maybe I can help you make a start."

She looked very carefully at me, directly into my eyes, impressing her need into me. Searching to see if I could be trusted. Would I avert my eyes? Acknowledging the failure to be what she needs. I let her eyes roam through my skull. "All right. What do I have to do?"

"Do you want to live at home anymore?"

"No way."

"Okay, then this is the deal. You go to a boarding school until you're eighteen. You get into therapy."

"Why?" she whined.

"Because this whole bag of shit has got to have affected you. Look at what you agreed to do to yourself with Tony. You need protection from yourself right now. To sort out what you've learned from all this and that takes somebody to do it with. That's why."

She looked sullenly at me as if I'd promised her a car and she found out it had no engine.

"Your dad will pay for the therapy, the school and all it costs, your clothes and that's it. No presents. No treats. No gifts. No bribes to come home. No little surprises because you've been so good. You want to have a good time, you pay your own way. You get a job in the summers."

"Why? He's got lots of money. He oughta owe me something for what he did."

"He does. He owes you plenty but none of it costs a cent. You can't take a bill for your pain to him and collect for it. He owes you, nobody else does. If he won't try to right things with you nobody else has to or can. What you've been through doesn't exempt you from future shit or entitle you to special treatment. If you survive your past, you get a future just like everyone else."

I sat back. "That's my offer. You stay in school until you're eighteen and in therapy until your therapist says you're done and your father picks up the tab. At eighteen you can do what you want. You understand?"

She nodded.

"Maybe someday you'll get to feel like those kids you saw on the street."

I thought that if I could wrap her in the trappings of childhood, school, friends, dances, homework, rules, an orderly flow of growing up with someone to help her sort herself out she might yet feel okay about herself and not so alone or bad. Who knows?

"I still don't know what I have to do."

"Yeah. Here comes the hard part." I told her what she needed to do to effect her escape. She chewed her thumb throughout. I thought of foxes' gnawed limbs left in spring traps and wondered how much of herself she'd have to leave behind to get free and whether it was any improvement on the law.

She sat and stared at me from a long way away, appraising me, cataloging me with a direct calm I hadn't seen before. I felt uncomfortable. The order of things was subtly shifting. I wasn't in charge here, setting down terms, getting my way. Yeah, getting my way. C'mon, kid, play along in my movie. See, I ride this white horse. No, we don't have to do that yucky stuff but we still do it my way. A master still. Benign, I hope, but just another master. Tough shit, the kid needed one right now.

She continued to look at me.

"Well, what do you say? Is it a deal or not?"

"Let me think about it."

More silent staring, eyes roving over me, a smirk sneaking across her mouth.

"Can I ask you a question?"

"Sure."

"What's in it for you?"

"You catch on quick. Good. What do I get? I get a chance to feel good about myself. That maybe I helped you get a chance to enjoy your life. It's the only one you get; make the best of it."

"Why bother?"

"Because I hate to see people hurt like that. I can't stand not being able to do anything about it." This was getting harder by the minute. "Because I know what it's like to feel like that. Shit. I don't know. I just do." I thought, You could say thank you, you little shit. I stared back at her. I continued trying to answer her question to myself and got nowhere. For thanks you live a long and happy life or I'll feel cheated. You owe me. Look at what I did for you. You owe me nothing. I did it for me. All of the above. None of the above. Get it straight, stupid, or get out. If I wanted thanks I'd better tell her now or forever hold my peace. "If you do it, do it for yourself. It's the only engine that'll pull that load.

I slapped my palm on the table. "How about some food?" She nodded.

I returned to the meat and potatoes, lumped them together, wrapped them in Saran and put them back in the refrigerator. She had gone off to the living room and had looked at my albums. She held up a particularly grim piece of vinyl. *Broken English* by Marianne Faithfull. A thirty-three and a third rpm howl into the dark—riveting but not fun. I didn't think that Marie Osmond spoke to this kid. "Sure."

I looked around and regrouped. Spaghetti and meat sauce. I cleaned the skillet and put in some sliced sausage. On the other burner I diced and dumped onion and tomatoes in butter, garlic, salt, pepper and a pinch of sugar.

She was sitting cross-legged in front of the stereo with my headphones on. A pot of water was set to boil. Any minute I'd deliver a one pound baby fettuccini. I set to stirring the sauce and trying to coordinate the timing of this.

Sausage, sauce and pasta began to converge. I turned back to Randi and semaphored S-E-T T-H-E T-A-B-L-E. She looked at me as if I were more than fashionably nuts, took off the headset and we completed the conversation on audio.

"Come here. Test the pasta. Okay?"

She stood next to me. I held out a strand of pasta to her. "Bite it. If it's a little chewy but not doughy, it's done." She bit it, chewed it pensively and then sucked the remainder from my grasp. Smiling, she announced it was done.

I got the grated Parmesan, poured some milk for her and got a Guinness for myself. We ate steadily, silently like two big cats at a common carcass, eyeing each other between bites, poised for flight or fight.

She put down her fork, dabbed at her mouth and looked at me with that unnerving calm she had surveyed me with before. "I want to live here with you."

I almost purpled on my pasta. "What!"

"Well, why not?" she pleaded. "I'll go to school like you said and therapy. Why can't I stay here, huh? I'll do whatever you want. I'll be good. I'm smart and I can help around here."

"No way, kid. Out of the question. Totally impossible."

"Why? You like me, I know you do. Why are you doing all this for me?"

"Whoa, whoa, you've got it all wrong, kid. It just won't work."

"Why? You said you wanted to help me be normal. Well, normal is having a family. I don't have one. My father can't keep his hands off me. My mother hates me. Why can't you be my father? I don't want to live in some boarding school like, like—" she threw her hands up in dismay—"some I-don't-know what."

It was out, all of it. Sitting there between us, an ugly knot of need and desire and fear as compelling and comforting as a tumor. Shit, shit, shit. You get into people's lives and they just don't behave. They just don't accept what you want to give. It's never enough. They always want more.

I was spinning my fork on the plate like I was digging for core samples. Down it went with a deep sigh. I looked at her, the devastating reasonableness of her need: someone to love her and care for her. Everybody's birthright and nobody wants her. She was as inviting as a fumble but no one was on the field. I reached out for her hand.

"I just can't do it, Randi. I just can't. It is just too much."

"Tell me why. Maybe I can fix it, make it okay. You told me I'd have to do the hard thing to get myself out. Why can't you do the hard thing? Why not?"

How to tell her all the things I feel? To give each the proper weight in this recipe of wish and doubt, fear and longing. "Because it is too much. I don't want to be a father. That responsibility terrifies me. I won't do it if I can't do it right and I sure as hell won't get it right if I don't want to. You've already had it done wrong once; you don't need that twice."

"Give me a chance. It might not be so bad. You couldn't be as bad as what I've had. I'll settle for you."

"I'm just not big enough for the job. I'm not the man you want or need, Randi. I can maybe clear a space so you can find someone who can be that for you, but it's not me."

She didn't hear me. Her fingers had slipped from my grasp. She was falling away from me on the oblivion express. Our eyes locked all the way down.

"I'm sorry. I really am."

Anytime you come up against something you just can't fix, it stays with you forever. It's a little death, a taste of the big one waiting beyond. Each fragile wish that's crushed in the brute pestle of one's own limits yields a bitter sauce for life.

She pushed herself away from the table and walked away. "I'm not hungry any more. I just want to go lie down. Can I use your bed?"

"Sure. I'll be up if you want to talk any more."

She ambled off, the wobbly wavering walk of the dazed. I turned away to wash the dishes, then thought better of it. I looked around the house, as adrift as she was. This was one of those times I wished I still smoked. The baroque stylized ritual of shaking out the cigarette, tamping the end, putting it in your mough, flicking the lighter, setting it on fire, taking that first long drag. Everything would be slowed down by that, well in hand, centered. I went over to the living room, fell into a chair, got up and got some whiskey and fell back again, staring out at the lawn, hoping a spaceship would land soon.

Randi came out of the bedroom door wearing only my T-shirt,

her hair pulled up in back, hands on hip. "I can't sleep. Do you have any Valiums or anything I can take?"

"No, I don't. If you aren't tired stay up, read, listen to music or something."

"No, that's okay." She turned back into the dark.

"Good night, Randi." A rock into a pool.

I sipped my drink and planned tomorrow's action. My heart wasn't in it. I got up and called Samantha. She was in.

"Hi. I called a while ago."

"Oh. I just got in."

"We found her—the kid. She's over here right now."

"Have you told her parents?"

"No."

"Why not?"

"Because dear old dad has been putting it to her since she was god knows how old."

"Have you called the police?"

"No, I've talked to a lawyer I know. From what he told me that would just be a circus, with this kid being the freak show and damn little done to daddy."

"So let me guess—you're going to rescue this girl."

"I'm going to try, anyway."

"Jesus, do you think everyone is incompetent? That nobody can do anything right?"

"No, not incompetent, but the legal system isn't set up to handle this. You know that. You read the newspapers. So you have to make your own system."

"What are you going to do?"

I told her. She groaned.

"Magnificent. Lunatic but magnificent. I hope your horse is off-white."

"You got a better idea?" This was getting worse by the minute. I just wanted to tell her about how I felt leaving the kid in the lurch and here I am justifying the bigger fuckin' hammer school of family therapy.

"Let me try one more time. We probably can't do much with

the father in terms of punishment or therapy. The kid would be exposed to a real horror show in court and then shunted off to a foster home until the department of social services returned her home, which is whenever the paperwork turns yellow." She started to speak. "Wait. You know what I mean, ten or twenty workers each with a caseload in the hundreds. They get reinvolved when there's screaming, blood and flashing lights, otherwise file it under Forgotten. I know it can't be any other way. You need six social workers to work 'round the clock to undo every family failure. Anyway, this way we can keep the kid's exposure private, protect her from her father and have some leverage over him to support her and put her in a place where she can sort out her life. I think it's an improvement over the other alternatives and I know all about Daddy's civil rights. Fuck 'em. That why I'm not a lawyer. All sides are not equal."

"What about the cost to this child of doing what you've suggested? That's a terrible position to put her in."

"I know it is. I can't think of any other way to find out whether or not the situation is salvageable. If it's not she's better off finding out at thirteen than wasting years trying to recreate a family she never had."

"You've put yourself in jeopardy for this kid in half a dozen ways."

"I know, I know. If this blows up I'll get to write my prison memoirs: *Pissed Off: In the Bladder of the Beast.* That's the chance you take."

"Why do it for this kid? Do you care that much?"

"Shit, does everybody carry an involve-o-meter on how much do you care?" I was airborne, fully armed. Destroy all life forms.

"Hey, Leo, what was that all about?"

I struggled to abort the mission. "That—" teeth unclenching "—was what this kid wanted to know. She asked if she could stay with me, and when I said no she really pushed on it. That spot is real tender right now."

"What did you expect her to do? You ride into her life, promising her all these changes in her life but the most important one: a man she can respect and trust to care for her. Why shouldn't she ask for it? You're giving her what you want, not what she most needs. Good for her."

"No, not just what I want to give her. That may be what you and I are trying to sort out: What I want to give of myself. But I *know* I'm not up to the task of being what this kid needs. And not misleading her is more important than not disappointing her. And I feel like shit about that right now. I called to ask if you'll help me. I think this kid is going to need some support when this is over. I need someone she can stay with for a couple of days while we find a school for her and I don't think I'm the person for that. Will you help me? If the police come looking for Randi, I asked you to take care of my niece for a couple of days. That's all you know."

"Shit. You don't ask much, do you? Let me think about it. When do you need to know?"

"It goes down tomorrow."

"Wonderful. I'll call you back later. Listen, just one question: Is this what life is like with you?"

"No, this is just an unusually smooth period I'm going through."

"I thought so. I'll call back."

I put down the phone. Randi was in the doorway. "I couldn't sleep." She hugged her shoulders. "I'll do what you want." Then slowly, "Will you write to me at school? Can I visit you sometimes, like holidays, maybe?"

"Yeah. I'd like that Randi. You'd better try to get some sleep. Tomorrow is going to be a long day."

"Who was that you were talking to?"

"A friend of mine, a woman, I think you'd like her. She's a good person. She'll be with us, I think. She's thinking it over now."

Randi crossed the room, stood on tiptoe, threw her arms around my neck and kissed my cheek. I flapped my arms like a wounded mallard, gave in and squeezed her back. I disentangled myself.

"Good night, Randi."

"Good night, Leo."

Samantha called back in a half hour and said she'd help. I went over the plan with her. I sat up a while and talked with Arnie, finalizing things. Later on I went to the bathroom to get some more aspirin. One of my razor blades was out on the sink. I left it there, a marker on the road.

I slept well until 3 A.M. I'd had a dream that I was driving across the desert. A pretty girl was hitchhiking on the side. I asked her if I could give her a ride. She kept trying to say thank you but no words came out of her mouth. Only blood.

Chapter 21

THE PHONE JERKED ME AWAKE. "MR. HAGGERTY, THIS IS LIEUTEN-ant Frank Schaefer of the Fairfax County Police Department. I would like you and that pet gorilla of yours to present yourselves at headquarters today, say 1 P.M., to answer some questions about the deaths of Teresa NMI Johnson and one Leroy Alfonso Dixon. Do you understand me?" When I said nothing Frank repeated himself a bit louder, then said, "Did you hear me?"

I was getting numb rapidly. "Yeah, I hear you." Then, "Frank, tell me one thing and don't lie to me."

"What?"

"Did she die alone?"

"No, Leo. She didn't die alone. She died in the ambulance."

"Thanks, Frank."

"Leo, be there at one. I don't want to have to put an APB out on you."

"We'll be there." Rest in peace, Terri. Rest in peace. I went into the bedroom and shook Randi awake. "Wake up. We've got things to do. We don't want to be late."

She rolled away from me. I went into the bathroom and cleaned myself up. I went back to the bedroom and pulled out a loose, cotton pullover shirt and wrapped it around some other things and went back to the bathroom.

Randi sat up and said, "What should I wear?"

"It doesn't matter. Something easy to get into. That shirt and a pair of my shorts. We'll get you some clothes later today." I went into the bathroom and locked the door. I unrolled the shirt and put the Beretta in its ankle holster and pulled my pants leg down over it. I was just going through the motions.

Randi sat on the bed. I said, "Go in and wash up. We'll be ready to go soon."

She looked up at me. "I'm scared."

"I know. It'll work out. We'll all be with you. It'll be over in a flash. There are no easy ways out of hard places." Reassure yourself, big fellah.

"I know and I'll do it. I'm just scared. He's my father you know."

"I know. I don't believe it but I know. Go get cleaned up."

She came out in a couple of minutes. We went into the kitchen and shared some salvaged hash from last night with fried eggs on top, croissants with lemon curd and fresh hot coffee. "One more thing, Randi. It may turn out the police will want to ask you some questions about what happened in the film place. It has nothing to do with you. It's because I killed that man. I don't want you to lie for me. You tell them what you want. You can tell them the truth. I'll take my chances. Do you understand?" She nodded yes. As we finished eating, Arnie pulled into the driveway.

"Okay, Randi, let's go." I locked up and we hustled out to the car. Randi slipped into the back seat. I got in next to Arnie. We backed into the street, the 454 cubic inch engine growling the whole way, barely restrained.

Arnie asked where to.

"Those little cabins off Route 1. Plenty of privacy. Nobody would notice if one of the buildings grew wings and took off."

"Fine. You got the gear?"

"Yeah, it's in the back."

We drove in silence down to the motel. Randi lay down in the back seat. Arnie paid for the room and we rolled down to it. It was the far end unit. We got out. The door was visible from the office. Arnie went back to chat up the owner and I hustled Randi into the room. There was a knock on the door.

"Yes."

"It's me, Leo. Let me in."

I pulled open the door. Samantha was in the doorway.

"Nice to see you. Randi, this is Samantha Clayton. Samantha, this is Randi Benson. Randi, when this is over you're going to stay for a few days at her apartment until we get things squared away for you. Samantha, buy her whatever things she needs to stay with you. I'll pick up the tab."

I left the two of them sitting on the side of the bed to survey the room's layout. It would do just fine. Arnie came back to the door, knocked and entered. "Ready to go?" he asked.

"Yeah. You and Samantha sit in your cars. Keep low. Benson's a big, beefy guy with a handlebar mustache. When he comes in, give it a good ten count then cross to the door and wait, okay?"

"Fine." Arnie and Samantha left.

I looked at Randi. "Hang tough, kid. They'll be right there for you. We won't let anything happen. If it goes like I think it will, you'll see you had to do it. I know you aren't crazy about it but I don't think there's any other way to end it."

She just sat there, looking at me with those eyes. Telling me I wouldn't believe how shitty life could be and wondering whether anything would be any better after this. I squeezed her hand. "Ready?"

She nodded. I left her there. I walked down to the public phone outside the manager's office.

"Hello."

"Yes, Mr. Benson, this is Leo Haggerty. I've got your daughter Randi. She's okay but she's been through a lot. I think you ought to come down here and get her right away."

"Where are you?"

I gave him the address of the motel and the cabin number. "I'm keeping her here; the manager doesn't know. Listen, hurry. I've got to try to put the lid on something so the police aren't involved. If you're coming right away, I'll leave her here for you to pick up. It's only a five-minute drive. She's ready to come home."

"Yeah, yeah, I'll be right over. She say anything to you?"

"What about?" Twist, pump the blade.

"Oh, you know, where she's been. What she's been doing."

"No, she's pretty closemouthed. Hasn't said much of anything."

"Yeah. I'm on my way."

I hung up and walked back to number fourteen. The stage was set. I took my position and waited. He was right on time. There was a knock on the door.

"Miranda?"

"Yes."

"Open up—it's Dad."

"It's unlocked. Come on in." She barely got the words out and was beginning to slump. She was losing the fight with herself. Her father slid into the room, looking both ways and locked the door behind him. He went to where she sat on the bed.

"Are you okay?"

Randi nodded head down. She couldn't look at him.

"That detective—did you tell him anything?"

Her head swung slowly, sadly from side to side.

"Good. That's my girl. Listen, I don't know what made you run away but we'll work it out. You just tell me what you want and it's yours. You want to stay out later with your friends, I understand. I've been thinking about it that maybe I've been too strict on you. Just, you know, I've been worried that it might slip out what's happened. You just promise me you'll forget about all this and we'll go home and start all over and everything'll be fine."

Randi looked up at him and nodded. Paralyzed like a rat dancing with a hawk. He looked down at her. Crossroads time. He dipped his head and kissed her below the ear like a vampire. She went rigid, her eyes closed.

"Just one last time," he croaked.

He pulled up her T-shirt and began to squeeze her breast. He stood over her, pushed her onto her back and brought her knees up and began to pull down her shorts. She rolled her head over in my direction, pleading with her eyes. I pushed open the door and Benson looked right at me and the camera. I kept on shooting all the way into the room. "Hold it right there, you son of a bitch."

Benson pushed her away and sprang for the door. He pulled it open and Arnie filled the doorway with his empty steel eyes, a metallic menace. Samantha slipped by them and ran up to Randi. She wrapped her up in a long coat and helped her up off the bed. Randi moved like a zombie. Samantha pushed Randi's head down onto her chest and averted her face from her father. Arnie pushed him back into the room with his palm and Randi slipped through the doorway. I retrieved the mini-recorder from the trash can in the corner of the room and put it into my pocket.

"Sit down, Mr. Benson."

He turned to me, glaring. "You scumbag! You filthy pervert! What are you going to do with those pictures? I can't believe she'd sink to this level so fast. I'm her father," he bellowed. "How could she do this to me?"

Awestruck, I looked at him, an engine of such colossal narcissism that no one else existed but that they furthered or thwarted his plans. The remonstration of others was persecution. All excess was justified.

"Sit down, Mr. Benson."

"What did you offer her, that slut, that . . . ?"

I helped Mr. Benson instantly assume the fetal position. "Keep your mouth shut, Benson. That's if you want to talk again in the next six weeks. I have had it with you. You're going to get up and sit on this bed very quietly and answer all of my questions or what you just got is going to become a regular occurrence. Are we in accord?"

He nodded.

"You set me up in the movie theater with those goons, right?"

He still didn't understand. "If I ask you again, Mr. Benson, your answers will be limited to nodding and crying. Are we communicating?"

"Yes."

"Excellent."

"Yes. I hired the guys to warn you off. I hired you to satisfy my wife. I wanted to get you to drop the case. I'd have found her eventually."

"Consider that first shot on behalf of a girl I jumped all over because of you. You've got a lot of accounts to settle. Now we come to your daughters. This is the deal and listen good. They both go away to school, away from you until they're eighteen. You foot the bill for school, necessities and therapy. You keep away from them both unless their therapist okays it. You don't buy anything else for them: no cars, no trips, no stereos. When Tammy's eighteen the deal is over and I destroy the tape and photos. You fuck up and this goes out in the mail to everyone you've ever met. Do we have an agreement?"

He nodded. "What'll I tell my wife?"

"That's your problem. The truth hasn't been much esteemed between you two before; I'm sure it won't be missed now."

"What's in it for you?"

"My bill promptly paid will suffice. Mr. Benson, I sincerely do not want to see or hear from you again. I'll contact you when the plans are worked out for Randi and Tammy. Oh, one more thing. The police may contact you about the work you hired me to do. Just tell them the truth. They may want you to notify them if Miranda shows up. If so, I'll call you to let you know when she's ready to talk to them. And don't worry; it's not about you. Your secret is still safe. You may leave now."

He sat there for a moment, lost in his new life. He slowly got up and turned to me. "Listen, you gotta understand, I didn't . . ."

"Don't tell me. I don't care. Whatever your story is, it doesn't excuse what you did. I'm not interested in understanding you. Just get out."

He opened the door and the morning sun flooded in. He went out and passed by Arnie's android gaze. I looked around at the room one last time. If I ever get to see the far side of hell I'm sure this room will be there.

I got off the bed, looked at Arnie and pulled the door closed behind me, flicking off the light. We walked together across the lot. I checked my watch. We had time to rehearse our story before our rendezvous with Frank Schaefer. I pointed over to Samantha's car and he nodded.

I walked over to the car, put my head in the window. "Randi, your dad has agreed to all the terms. You'll stay with Samantha until we get a school lined up for you. We're going to take care of Tammy too. I know things feel bad right now, but I think the worst is over. I'll be in touch with you, okay?"

She looked up, huddled in the blanket, her face furrowed by tear tracks and nodded dully at me.

I looked at Samantha. "Thanks for being there. Arnie and I have to see the police about some things that happened to the guys that had Randi. I'll see you when we're done."

She nodded. I looked at her, memorizing her face, more sure than ever that I didn't want to lose her. Not to evil or accident, microbes or men, and most of all not to my own fears.

She looked back at me steadily, intently. I kissed her lightly on the lips. She drove off and I stood alone in the lot, feeling both larger and smaller than before.

Chapter **22**

AFTER A BRIEF STOP AT THE COUNTY LAND OFFICE ARNIE AND I walked into the police station at one o'clock sharp and were shown into Frank Schaefer's office. He looked up as we walked in. "Well, if it isn't Fairfax County's very own A-Team. Sit down."

We drew up chairs, sat and stared at Frank across his desk. He tented his fingers.

"As you can see there's no stenographer here and I'm going to question the two of you together, so this is a very informal inquiry. Anything you can tell us to solve these two murders will be greatly appreciated."

"Go ahead, Frank. What do you want to know?"

"We went out on your say-so to the house on Lorton Church Road and found Teresa Johnson. She confirmed what you had said, that Leroy Dixon had raped and attacked her. She lost consciousness after that. Can you tell us why Dixon would want her dead?"

"Dixon and another guy, Tony Julian, were ripping off Monte Panczak. They tumbled to the fact that she wasn't just a working girl and assumed that she was working for Panczak. They killed her to keep her quiet."

"What were you doing out at that house, Leo?"

"She'd called me the night before and told me she might have some information about the missing kid I was looking for."

"And why would she do that?"

"We'd crossed paths earlier when it looked like Tony Julian might have been seen with the kid. I figured out that she was up to something other than hooking. She told me she was a reporter doing a story and I asked her to keep her eyes open, that's all."

"Yeah, that's all. Now you need two pennies to keep her eyes closed."

"That's a cheap shot, Frank, and you know it." I was halfway up out of my chair.

"You're damn right I know it and I'm going to stick you with it anyway because I know you're lying to me even if I can't ever prove it and I want you to know that I know." His finger shook as he pointed it at me. "You got anything you want to tell me that'll make me think otherwise?"

I shook my head no.

"You may get away with grandstanding in North-fucking-Carolina, but you're on notice here, Leo. You can't play me for a chump. You live here and you work here. I hope you know better than to shit where you eat."

"Finish your questions, Frank," I snapped.

Frank took a deep breath. He'd given me the mandatory warning and I knew he more than half meant it. He pulled out some Rolaids and fiddled with the wrapper.

"The Dixon thing is Alexandria's baby. Whoever did it was good and lucky. They didn't leave much to tag themselves with. Some clothing fibers on Dixon's body and a bloodstain on an office wall. No prints. Very professional piece of work. They even thought to disable the elevators. You know anybody that would think about something like that, Mr. Kendall?"

"Beats me."

"I'm sure it does. I did a little checking on you, sergeant. Arnie 'Can-do' Kendall, Medal of Honor winner. Your old commanding officer says there's nothing you can't do in the killing department. That so?"

Arnie just stared blankly at Frank. As in the restaurant Frank broke off his gaze first. Shaking his head he went on. "You knew where this film lab was. You didn't stay put at the firehouse like I asked you to. I'm sure that if Alexandria hustles on this one, they'll find somebody who can put you two in the right place at the right time. That's opportunity. How does revenge sound as a motive to you, Leo?"

"Sounds like you're reaching, Frank. If that's all they've got I'm not going to lose any sleep over this. If you guys come up with something substantial like an eyewitness or a murder weapon, let me know." I leaned back in my chair and studied Frank's face. The three Vs under his eyes grew even whiter as his cheeks flushed a deeper red.

"I told you these guys got lucky too. The bullet that blew off the back of Dixon's head ricocheted off the steel door of the stockroom and was so badly flattened that ballistics couldn't do anything with it. We do know it was a .45 ACP slug. You favor that, don't you, Leo?" He held up his hands. "I don't even want to know." After unrolling his antacid pills he popped one in his mouth and chewed it up.

"There was a witness too. Tony Julian, how about that? He didn't actually see the guys. He heard them fighting with Dixon about a drug buy he supposedly stiffed them on. He tried to get away to get help, slipped on the staircase and got knocked out. When he came to he was tied up and they were gone. Convenient, eh?"

"That's it, Frank? As far as I can tell Terri Johnson was killed by Leroy Dixon who in turn was killed by unknown drug dealers. I thought Tony Julian knew something about the kid I was looking for. Terri Johnson thought so too. That's why I was out there at the house. Beyond that I don't really see how we figure in this, Frank, do you?"

"No, I guess not, Leo. But why don't you do me a favor and stay downwind of me for a while until I forget about Terri Johnson. Now get out."

Arnie and I got up and left. I thought about telling Frank how sorry I was about what had happened but there was no way to explain myself and what I had done or not done without opening more wounds than I'd close. He was damn angry with me and if he really thought I'd gotten Terri Johnson killed he'd never have anything to do with me. He had enough doubts to tell me what Alexandria had on the Dixon killing.

In a phone booth on Route 1 I called Monte Panczak. After the usual runaround I got the great one himself.

"Mr. Panczak. This is your friend. I'm just calling to tell you that I've recovered what your employees took from me. I'm sure you've read about the unfortunate deaths of Mr. Dixon, whom I understand you knew slightly, and a Miss Teresa Johnson. You might wish to go over the wooded property you own that adjoins the house on Lorton Church Road. Mr. Dixon was very sloppy in a housecleaning operation of his own and left some debris on your property."

"Thank you for that information, friend. I am on my way out to that property right now. I have plans to do some planting on those fields."

Chapter **23**

I TOLD ARNIE I'D BE IN TOUCH WITH HIM AND DROVE ON TO Samantha's place. I trudged up the stairs to her unit on the top floor of a three story garden apartment building. No one had gotten out unscathed in this one. I leaned on the door bell for a second and then straightened up. Samantha opened the door. She was dressed all in khaki, with lots of pockets, snaps and zippers on her blouse and shorts.

"Going on safari?"

"No need to. All the wild things just seem to come to my door." She opened it wider and I walked in.

"Where's Randi?"

"Sleeping. She was so keyed up when I brought her in we just talked for hours. She finally relaxed enough to go to sleep and she conked out on my bed.

"Would you like a drink?" she asked.

"Yeah."

"Irish, neat. Yes?"

"Yes."

She went into the kitchen and came back with a glass for each of us.

"What does it mean that I'm starting to keep Irish whiskey on hand?"

"It means that your taste in whiskey is improving. I don't know what it says about the company you keep."

I took the glass from her and sat down in an overstuffed sofa.

"How did it go?" she asked.

"It went. I'm pretty sure Randi has been kept out of it. I could conceivably be indicted for Leroy Dixon's death but I doubt it. You don't want to know about the rest of it, but I think I fixed it."

"I do want to know about the rest of it. I'm involved, remember? Randi told me what happened at the film place. What else is there?"

"What else is there?" I looked into her face: the large brown eyes, the wide mouth I'd so wanted the first time I had seen her. Then it was her desire I wanted. Now it was her understanding. One woman, all things.

"I'll tell you. In a wooded field down in Lorton, Arnie and I killed four men. I cut the throat of a boy not terribly much older than Randi. He didn't leave me any choice. They were there to kill us."

I stopped and downed half my drink. It burned going down but cauterized nothing. I looked at her. She was leaning forward, hands pressed together. Just listening, just there.

"A woman, a good woman I think, got killed. It was a very ugly death. That's it." I drained the rest of my drink and thought about all the losses. Samantha got up, walked over and sat down next to me. She worked her hands into mine.

"No, that's not it. That's not all there is."

"Oh yeah?" I said. "What else is there?"

"I found you and you found me."